Having a Wonderful Time, Wish You Were Her

by Billy Van Zandt
and
Jane Milmore

A SAMUEL FRENCH ACTING EDITION

SAMUEL FRENCH

FOUNDED 1830

New York Hollywood London Toronto

SAMUELFRENCH.COM

"HAVING A WONDERFUL TIME, WISH YOU WERE HER" was first presented at the Dam Site Dinner-Theatre, Tinton Falls, New Jersey. Opening Night: Friday, June 11, 1982. It was directed by William Van Zandt. It was produced by Kathy Reed. Set and lighting design were by Russell Schiavone. Stage Manager was Jennifer Milmore. Costumes were by Jane Milmore. The cast, in order of appearance, was as follows:

KATHY . . . . *Pamela D'Amato*
DANNY . . . . *Billy Van Zandt*
JENNIFER . . . . *Jane Milmore*
PAUL. . . . . *Tom Frascatore/Michael Terzano*
MARY . . . . *Judy Newcomb*
BILL . . . . *Don Brennan*

HAVING A WONDERFUL TIME
WISH YOU WERE HER

ACT ONE

Scene One

(CURTAIN RISES on a hotel room. At the center of the room is a double bed with two night tables. S.L. we see a desk and a chair. A telephone sits on one of the night tables. the curtains behind the bed are drawn. The door U.S.R. opens to reveal a COUPLE locked in a passionate kiss. THEY enter the room, beelining for that bed. The man carries a box in one arm and a bowling ball in the other. Never breaking the kiss, THEY kick the door shut behind them and proceed to the bed, undressing as THEY kiss and speak. Both DANNY and KATHY are in their late twenties. DANNY appears successful and in control, a firm believer in any double standard. KATHY is an attractive red-head, who appears to live only for moments like this.)

KATHY. *(breathy)* I missed you, Danny. This past week has been hell without you.

DANNY. *(breathy)* It was hard to get away. I missed you too.

KATHY. *(breathy)* I want you, Danny.

DANNY. And you'll get me. Let me get my jacket off, first. *(DANNY pulls his jacket off and flings it over his shoulder.)*

KATHY. Forever, Danny. I want you forever.

DANNY. And I want you. *(checks his watch)* But we only have until eleven. *(DANNY starts to kiss her. KATHY stops him short with her hand.)*

KATHY. Eleven? I thought she was going to a double-feature.

DANNY. Who can sit through two Jerry Lewis movies in one night? Be reasonable. *(HE starts to kiss her. KATHY stops him again.)*

KATHY. That only gives us two and a half hours!

DANNY. Yes, but it's two and a half hours of bliss.

KATHY. I'm tired of sneaking around. I want to be able to go out in public with you. I want to let the world see how much I love you. I'm sick of hiding behind menus and wearing these stupid wigs. *(KATHY pulls off her red hair. Long blond hair falls down on her shoulders.)*

DANNY. You look good in wigs. Especially that curly brown one that makes you look like Jacqueline Bisset. *(checks his watch)* Did you happen to bring that one with you tonight? *(DANNY reaches for her shoulder bag to check for the wig. HE is slapped away.)*

KATHY. No! And stop looking at your watch! You are so paranoid! You timed the drive over here. You timed the elevator ride up to the room. What else do you plan on timing tonight? Does your watch have a second hand?

DANNY. You gave it to me. I was just admiring it.

KATHY. Then let me wear it. You can admire me.

DANNY. I adore you. You know that. *(removing her*

scarf) You're the only woman in my life. The only woman that matters to me. I worship you.

KATHY. What about your wife?

DANNY. What about her?

KATHY. She is very much in your life. You spend a big two and a half hours a week with me and she gets you the rest of the time.

DANNY. Yeah, but who says I enjoy it? We've been through this before. This is the wrong time for me to get divorced. It will be too messy and I can't afford a scandal. Just give me some more time. Besides, this would destroy her right now and I don't want that on my conscience.

KATHY. (*SHE'S been through this many times.*) I don't want to hurt her either.

DANNY. I brought you a present. Here. (*HE hands her box from the bed*)

KATHY. You remembered. I knew you'd remember.

DANNY. I did? What did I remember?

KATHY. It's our year and a half anniversary. You knew that.

DANNY. Ah yes . . . I was testing you. I like to think of it as our eighteen month anniversary.

(*KATHY opens the box and takes out a sexy corset.*)

KATHY. Ooh, how sexy. (*SHE holds it up to her body.*) Is this a present for you or me?

DANNY. It was either this one or the one with the tassles. . . .

(*KATHY tips box and shakes it.*)

KATHY. That's it?

DANNY. I wanted to get you more, but our radiator cracked on the Toyota and we had new rugs put in the den on Wednesday . . .

KATHY. It's beautiful. I'll go try it on. (*SHE kisses him. Lusting after him.*) I love you . . . Danny Boy.

DANNY. (*breathy*) I love you . . . Poot.

KATHY. I'll be right back. (*SHE slinks off U.S.L. with her corset. DANNY sneaks a peek at his watch.*)

DANNY. (*calling to her*) Don't be long. (*DANNY immediately takes off his vest and shoes, throwing them on the bed. HE pulls off his pants, revealing boxers underneath. His pants also get thrown on the bed. HE then checks his watch, grabs his suit jacket and fishes in the breast pocket. HE takes out a piece of paper with a phone number. HE goes to phone, checks his watch one more time and dials. Whispering*) Hello. Is this the Carlton Theater? What time does "The Big Mouth" get out? . . . The movie! (*checks his watch*)

(*KATHY enters from the bathroom in her corset and black stockings. SHE poses across the room.*)

KATHY. What are you doing, dialing Time?

DANNY. Dial-a-Prayer.

KATHY. (*posing*) Well?

DANNY. Next week she goes to "Gone With the Wind." I promise.

(*THEY meet mid-way and attack each other.*)

KATHY. (*between kisses*) Oh, I have to switch next week to Tuesday. Is that a problem?

DANNY. (*kissing her*) We can talk about it later. In the car. Of course it's no problem. you change your schedule for me all the time. You have to work?

KATHY. (*out of breath*) No. But I made plans already.

DANNY. Going out with one of your stewardess friends?

KATHY. No. You're right. We can discuss it in the car, later. I've missed you so much.

DANNY. Who are you going out with? That fat girl?

KATHY. It's nothing special. Just some guy I went to college with.

(*DANNY freezes. KATHY continues kissing his neck as THEY sit on the bed.*)

DANNY. Wait a minute.

KATHY. (*looking down into his lap*) What's wrong?

DANNY. Wait-a-minute!

KATHY. What's the matter?

(*DANNY rises in shock. HE begins pacing.*)

DANNY. I didn't hear you correctly. I thought I heard you say that you were going out with "some guy."

KATHY. That's what I did say. Oh, Danny, don't act so ridiculous. It's no big romance. Just a guy I've been seeing.

DANNY. "Been seeing?" "Been seeing?" You've already gone out with him?

KATHY. Just for a couple of weeks. Make love to me. (*KATHY poses back on the bed, very invitingly. DANNY steps up to her.*)

DANNY. How many weeks?

KATHY. What's the difference?

DANNY. "What's the difference?" (*pacing again*) "What's

the difference?" When I started this relationship I expected commitment, that's the difference!

KATHY. (*rising*) How can you say that? You're married!

DANNY. That's different.

KATHY. I'm in love with you.

DANNY. Are you sleeping with him?

KATHY. Danny . . .

DANNY. KATHLEEN . . . ARE YOU SLEEPING WITH HIM?

KATHY. I'm not going to answer that.

DANNY. (*pacing*) I knew it. I knew it. You are sleeping with him!

KATHY. Danny, what did you expect me to do? Just sit at home and do nothing but wait for you to call, so I can enjoy myself two hours out of every week? Like some kind of a call girl or a kept woman?

DANNY. (*slight pause*) Yes!

KATHY. How dare you! (*KATHY throws his clothes and shoes at him. DANNY dodges and catches them as they fly through the air.*)

KATHY. Get out!

DANNY. That's not what I meant. You should never have told me this.

KATHY. Why should this change anything?

DANNY. Because it's wrong, that's why.

KATHY. "Wrong?" Get over here.

(*DANNY obeys, meeting her in front of the bed, setting his belongings back down on the bed behind him.*)

KATHY. Why is it wrong for me to see another man? You do it.

DANNY. I've never seen another man in my life.

KATHY. You sleep with another woman.

DANNY. That's different. I have to sleep with her. She's my wife.

KATHY. So, why is it wrong for me?

DANNY. (*without an answer*) Because . . . (*pacing and turning back to her*) in the eyes of God, it is wrong.

KATHY. "In the eyes of God?" "In the eyes of God?" Why is it all right for a man to sleep around, but wrong for a woman?

DANNY. Aha!! So you ARE sleeping with him! I knew it! I knew you acted differently. Besides, I do not sleep around. You, and her, and that's it. I know the meaning of the word "control."

KATHY. I can't believe you. This is a side of you I've never seen.

DANNY. Ha, I know what side you're interested in. I should have seen this coming. Any woman who will sleep with a married man cannot be trusted.

(*KATHY knocks the wind out of him and HE crumples
    TO THE BED.*)

KATHY. That's not fair. I am in love with you. I fought off this relationship for a very long time. You seduced me. You remember that? You seduced me!

DANNY. (*rising*) I would hardly call dinner by candlelight at "Windows on the World," flowers, a ride through Central Park under the stars in a horsedrawn carriage, a suite at the Plaza and three quaaludes a seduction.

KATHY. I didn't think you'd react like this.

DANNY. And when I think of my wife, who trusts me, as I trusted you, sitting there, alone, watching "The Big Mouth" . . . . it almost makes me want to cry. For the past two years I have lived only for you. Do you think I like giving up my bowling night every week? Of course not. But I do it for you. Because I love you. And this is the thanks I get. I've given you the best Monday nights of my life. And for what? To be cast aside for a college graduate. Let me tell you something about college . . .

KATHY. Well, what about me? I've practically lived like a nun for the past two years . . .

DANNY. (*pointing to her corset*) Ha!

(*KATHY makes another fist and DANNY shuts up.*)

DANNY. Continue.

KATHY. I never thought a casual date now and then would make you react like this.

DANNY. Well, we're both learning a great deal about each other tonight, aren't we?

KATHY. Danny, are you going to make love to me or not?

DANNY. How can you even ask me that?

KATHY. Because I want to make love to you.

DANNY. Why, is your college friend taking night courses?

KATHY. Get out of here! (*KATHY begins pelting DANNY with his clothing and shoes again.*) You can't take it, can you? It's perfectly all right for me to think about you and her in bed together all the time . . . but when the shoe's on the other foot . . .

DANNY. That's where I want my shoes. On my feet. Not in my face.

KATHY. If it'll make you feel any better, you're better in bed.

DANNY. That has absolutely nothing to do with it!

(*pause*) How much better?

KATHY. I could never find another man like you.

DANNY. I know that and you know that. But tell him!

KATHY. You know there could never be anyone else in the world for me . . . kiss me. (*posing at bed*) Don't you find me sexy? . . . Danny Boy?

(*KATHY puckers and DANNY closes in for the kiss. HE changes his mind and crosses away in a huff.*)

KATHY. Now what's wrong?

DANNY. Don't you touch me.

KATHY. What?

DANNY. You don't love me. You've never loved me. You only want me for my body. (*HE poses his pathetic body.*)

KATHY. You are a sick person. Do you know that?

DANNY. I'm going to the movies.

KATHY. Why?

DANNY. My marriage is a mess. And the one person I thought I trusted. The one person I thought I loved more than life itself has played me for a fool. I am going where I am loved and know I can trust. I'm going to a Jerry Lewis movie. (*DANNY gets dressed during the following.*)

KATHY. At least with him I don't have to hide. He's not ashamed of taking me out and being seen with me. Don't leave, Danny. I love you, and we still have time on the room.

DANNY. I'll always love you, Kathy. But this is wrong. And you're right. You deserve better. Only two and a half hours a week with me is hardly fair.

KATHY. It keeps me satisfied all week long.

DANNY. Really?

KATHY. If you decide you want me again, I'll be here.

(DANNY checks his watch.)

DANNY. We only have the room for another hour.

KATHY. It was a beautiful year and a half. *(indicating corset)* May I keep this?

DANNY. Yeah. I got it on sale anyway.

KATHY. I think you're making a mistake.

DANNY. *(eyeing her up and down)* Somehow I do, too.

(KATHY rushes up to kiss him goodbye. DANNY sticks out his hand. THEY shake. DANNY picks up his bowling ball and crosses to the door.)

KATHY. Promise me something.

(DANNY stops.)

Promise me you'll come back to me if things don't work out.

DANNY. *(stepping back in, sincerely)* I'll promise that. Promise me something.

KATHY. Anything.

DANNY. If he has a disease, you'll let me know!

KATHY. Get out!!

BLACKOUT

Scene Two

(*LIGHTS UP on a different hotel room. Much cheaper. A YOUNG COUPLE enters. THEY race in, slamming the door behind them. THEY are out of breath. THEY are JENNIFER & PAUL. PAUL is a nervous but confirmed bachelor. A lot cooler in his mind than in his manner. JENNIFER is a terrified girl-woman, naive and obedient and beautiful. BOTH wear trenchcoats, sunglasses and hats. PAUL sports a fake mustache.*)

PAUL. We made it! (*PAUL races to the drapes and peeks out to make sure THEY weren't followed. HE removes his coat and hat. HE checks the phone for wire-taps, which HE then takes off the hook. JENNIFER stands frozen at the door during all of it.*)

JENNIFER. We're going to get caught. I know it. We're going to get caught.

PAUL. (*racing to her side*) We're not going to get caught. I told you. With these sunglasses and this mustache, nobody will even look twice at us. (*HE unbuttons her coat*)

JENNIFER. It's nine-thirty at night, Paul. Who wears sunglasses at nine-thirty at night?

15

PAUL. Stevie Wonder. Would you relax? (*PAUL removes his fake mustache.*)

JENNIFER. How did you sign the register? You didn't sign anything obvious like Mr. & Mrs. Smith, did you?

PAUL. Of course not. I signed your husband's name.

JENNIFER. YOU DID WHAT?

(*PAUL races over to her, covering her mouth with his hand.*)

PAUL. He'll never think of looking under his own name. Relax.

JENNIFER. (*terrified*) I'm relaxed.

(*PAUL guides her into the room.*)

PAUL. Isn't this a lovely room?

JENNIFER. (*stopping short as SHE eyes the bed*) He must never find out, Paul. Ever. I've never cheated on him. We have been married for six years. I've never even looked at another man. Once the bag boy at Foodtown winked at me. . .

PAUL. And what happened?

JENNIFER. I shop at Pathmark now. I'm very loyal.

PAUL. That's what I love about you. (*PAUL removes her raincoat in a quickly executed smooth move. HE hangs it on a non-existent hook on the wall and it falls to the ground behind JENNIFER'S back.*)

JENNIFER. I was very proud at being the only faithful wife on the block.

PAUL. (*kissing her neck*) Yeah, you've got a nice neighborhood.

JENNIFER. (*still stiff, oblivious to his advances*) I believe in marriage, Paul.

PAUL. You can't call what you have a marriage, Jennifer. He neglects you. He ignores you. He makes you take the garbage out!

JENNIFER. You're right. I forgot what it was like to feel like a woman. Until you. You talk to me. You make me feel like a woman with feelings. Not just a sex machine. Five – six times a day. Every day.

PAUL. Yeah, I'm a great talker.

JENNIFER. Anything I say, you remember. You know, we have been married for six years and he still doesn't know my favorite perfume. He blames it on his deviated septum, but he just can't remember. Every birthday. Every special occasion, he brings me Charlie. I hate Charlie! I've got twenty-seven bottles of Charlie hidden at the bottom of my hamper. I can't bring myself to wear it and he can't smell anything anyway.

PAUL. What a thoughtless guy.

JENNIFER. What's my favorite perfume, Paul?

PAUL. Je Reviens.

JENNIFER. (*warming up*) How did you know?

PAUL. I've got a good memory and clear sinuses.

JENNIFER. Kiss me.

(*In a romantic move, PAUL lifts her up, and carries her to the bed in a passionate kiss. As HE sets her down, and THEY kiss, JENNIFER panics and throws him off her. PAUL falls off the bed onto the floor.*)

JENNIFER. Did you lock the door?

PAUL. (*in pain*)It's a hotel. The doors automatically lock in hotels.

JENNIFER. Put a chair in front of it, just to be safe?

PAUL. I'll put out the "Do Not Disturb Sign". (*HE heads for the door, discovering a severe limp from his fall which HE carries throughout the entire scene.*)

JENNIFER. Do we have to advertise it, Paul? Let's just get it over with and go home. (*JENNIFER lies back on the bed, stiff as a board preparing for the worst.*)

PAUL. (*taking in her new pose*) I'll use a chair. (*PAUL limps to the door, bracing it shut with a chair back.*) There. All locked. (*HE moves in to kiss her and JENNIFER bolts up, disgusted.*)

JENNIFER. Oh, I think I'm going to be sick. I hope this isn't a marathon session or I think I'll get sick.

PAUL. What?

JENNIFER. Let's try and make it real quick so I don't have time to think about it.

PAUL. I'll try.

JENNIFER. I wish I was drunk. I don't know if I can go through with this, Paul. Couldn't you have gotten me drunk first, so I'd have an excuse?

PAUL. I wish I was drunk so I'll have an excuse.

JENNIFER. (*picking up telephone*) Let's order up some drinks.

(*PAUL puts his hand on the telephone base.*)

PAUL. I don't want you drunk.

(*JENNIFER hangs up the phone, on PAUL'S hand.*)

JENNIFER. But you do want me?

(*PAUL rises, wincing in pain. His hand remains mangled through the entire scene. HE romantically throws off his shoes.*)

PAUL. I've wanted you for so long.

JENNIFER. And I've wanted you. But this is wrong. We should wait. (*SHE grabs her coat and heads for the door.*) That's what we'll do. We'll wait.

PAUL. (*diving across the bed, grabbing her by her coat*) Wait? Wait for what?

JENNIFER. (*tugging on her coat*) If you love me, you'll wait. He can't live forever. If you really love me, Paul, you'll wait fifty or sixty years for me to be free. (*JENNIFER tugs her coat free, flipping PAUL from bed to floor.*)

PAUL. He makes you wash the car, Jennifer.

JENNIFER. (*tossing coat over her shoulder*) To hell with him. Kiss me.

(*PAUL rises. JENNIFER puts out her arms, waiting to be picked up again. PAUL hobbles to her and lifts her, this time with difficulty. THEY kiss and proceed to the bed. Startled, JENNIFER throws PAUL off her. HE falls to the floor on his head.*)

JENNIFER. Paul, before we start . . . there's something I have to know.

PAUL. (*face down*) What?

JENNIFER. Am I just another notch on your bedpost? If I am, I can accept it, but I have to know.

(*PAUL climbs up, using his head.*)

PAUL. Jennifer, I swear, you are the only married woman I have ever wanted.

JENNIFER. Do you love me?

PAUL. (*posing romantically*) Yes.

JENNIFER. Will you love me forever?

PAUL. (*deeper*) Yes.

JENNIFER. (*testing him*) Would you take out the garbage for me?

PAUL. (*pausing romantically*) Even food scraps.

JENNIFER. Kiss me. (*SHE closes her eyes and holds out her arms. PAUL reacts at having to lift her again. HE picks her up, almost giving himself a hernia and throws her on the bed before HE drops her. HE goes to kiss her.*) Paul?

(*PAUL braces his body from possibly being thrown again.*)

PAUL. What?!

JENNIFER. How many women have you been with?

PAUL. What?

JENNIFER. How many women have you been with?

PAUL. I don't know. Jennifer, what kind of a guy do you think I am? I'm not like those kind of guys. I am a perfect gentleman. Any woman I have been to bed with has been a perfect lady. No cheap one night stands for me.

JENNIFER. How many, Paul?

PAUL. Fifty-seven. You make fifty-seven.

JENNIFER. When did you have time?

PAUL. I gave up racquetball.

JENNIFER. (*beginning to unbutton her blouse*) You're only the second man I'll ever have gone to bed with. My husband was the first.

PAUL. I figured that.

JENNIFER. I'm afraid. What if you don't like me?

PAUL. Don't be ridiculous. What's not to like?

JENNIFER. I don't have much stamina. My husband says I'm no fun after five or six hours.

PAUL. You did say you wanted it to be real quick, didn't you?

JENNIFER. You don't mind?

PAUL. No, if it'll make you happy.

JENNIFER. Until you, I'd almost forgotten what "happy" was. You make me feel so special.

PAUL. That's my specialty. (*PAUL pulls his sweater over his head, with difficulty.*)

JENNIFER. Take me home, Paul.

PAUL. (*dropping the sweater at his feet*) Now? We haven't done anything yet.

JENNIFER. This is wrong. I can't go through with this. He'll know.

PAUL. How will he know?

JENNIFER. (*crossing for the door*) I'll probably tell him.

PAUL. Jesus! Don't do that! (*PAUL runs after her, tripping on his sweater and falling on his face.*)

JENNIFER. I can't help it. I always tell him the truth. Even before he asks me things, I tell him things. I'm impulsive that way. (*In trying to stand, PAUL has been sitting on his right leg, HE looks around the floor wondering where HE lost it. HE claws his way into a standing position.*)

PAUL. For God's Sake, Jenny, you can't tell him!

JENNIFER. I'm not afraid anymore, Paul. I wouldn't be here tonight. You made me brave.

PAUL. I made you brave? And I'll make you a liar too. He can't ever find out, Jenny.

JENNIFER. Why not? You're not ashamed of me, are you?

PAUL. Of course not. But he's so trusting. (*suspicious*) He does trust you, doesn't he?

JENNIFER. Of course he trusts me. Why shouldn't he trust me?

PAUL. No reason. Let me put it another way. You wouldn't want to see me all beat up, would you?

JENNIFER. You're not afraid of him, Paul, are you? (*laughing*) If I didn't know any better, I'd swear you were afraid of him.

PAUL. (*cocky*) It's a good thing you know better. (*dropping to his knees and begging*) Please don't tell him. I just finished paying for new caps.

JENNIFER. For you, I'll lie.

(*PAUL rises, regaining his "suave" composure.*)

PAUL. You are so special. (*PAUL starts to kiss her, his face is pushed away. PAUL reacts to a dislocated jaw.*)

JENNIFER. Are you sure the door is locked?

PAUL. Reinforced with a chair and everything.

JENNIFER. There's only one thing to do then.

PAUL. I thought you'd never say it. (*PAUL drops his pants. JENNIFER turns away.*)

JENNIFER. Don't be disgusting, Paul. That's not what I meant. (*peeking through her fingers*) You really do love me, don't you?

(*PAUL poses romantically, arms out-stretched, pants around his feet*)

PAUL. More than you can ever know.

JENNIFER. And you'll never ignore me or leave me or hurt me.

PAUL. Never. (*PAUL begins crossing to her, with pants around his feet shortening his steps, with a severe limp, with a crushed hand and a bent shoulder.*)

JENNIFER. Then there's only one thing to do then. I'll get a divorce. (*JENNIFER crosses past PAUL for the door. HE follows, tripping on his pants and crashing to the floor.*)

PAUL. What? What would you want to do that for?

JENNIFER. So I can give myself to you freely.

PAUL. (*using the bed to climb up with his head*) What's the matter with tonight? I feel pretty free tonight.

JENNIFER. I'm still a married woman. You wouldn't want to make love to me like this. (*JENNIFER poses innocently, cleavage in his face.*)

PAUL. I'll force myself. (*PAUL resumes trying to get up, wrestling with his pants.*)

JENNIFER. As soon as I'm free of my marriage I can give myself to you openly and honestly.

(*PAUL rises, finally winning the war with his pants. HE throws them to the ground.*)

PAUL. What if he won't divorce you? What if he flat out refuses? Why would any man want to give up such perfection?

JENNIFER. I didn't think of that.

PAUL. Well, think of it! Think of it!

JENNIFER. But I don't know if I can live with myself if we sleep together.

PAUL. Sure you can. It's easy. After a while, you'll hardly remember any other way of life.

JENNIFER. How would you know? You said you were always loyal to your women.

PAUL. I heard stories. (*PAUL turns in to kiss her. JENNIFER pushes his face away, stepping forward. PAUL rubs his broken jaw.*)

JENNIFER. I have to go home, Paul.

PAUL. To what? Go home to what? To a man who makes you shingle the roof? To a man who listens to Ethel Merman records? To a man who buys you Charlie?

JENNIFER. What's my favorite color, Paul?

PAUL. Pink. Your favorite color is pink.

(*JENNIFER steps into the room.*)

JENNIFER. What's my favorite flower, Paul?

PAUL. (*disgusted*) Carnations. The long-stemmed pink ones.

JENNIFER. Oh, I don't know.

PAUL. Trust me.

JENNIFER. Are you sure you don't want to wait?

PAUL. Wait? I've watched you for over six years. Wanting you. Craving you. You have no idea what torture it's been everytime I see him touch you. My one desire was to die and come back reincarnated as your husband's hands. I fought this off, Jennifer. But the pain. The yearning. The cold showers. The pain of it all. This is mad to desire a married woman. It goes against all my principles. Theoretically, I'm a real shit. But I can't help myself. I'm a real shit and I'm glad! I love you . . . and if it means waiting fifty or sixty years for your husband to drop dead, all right then! I'll wait! But don't expect me to be faithful until then.

(*JENNIFER pulls the chair away from the door, as PAUL turns away, dejected and defeated.*)

PAUL. I knew it was too good to be true. Your being here tonight. (*Behind PAUL'S back, JENNIFER puts out the "Do Not Disturb" sign and crosses to the bed, undressing. PAUL assumes SHE'S gone.*) To think you'd leave that thoughtless miserable human being for me. The man who makes you shovel snow!
JENNIFER. Paul?
PAUL. What?
JENNIFER. Come to bed, Paul.
PAUL. You're kidding.
JENNIFER. Now.

(*PAUL crosses to her in his contorted, pained condition.*)

PAUL. (*sheepishly*) Be gentle with me.

BLACKOUT

Scene Three

(*LIGHTS UP on a bedroom somewhere in suburbia. We see an OLDER COUPLE in their mid-fifties; BILL & MARY. BILL: a stern looking man, sits in a chair watching a war movie on TV. HE wears a bathrobe, socks and a Marine flight hat. MARY, his wife, folds socks on the bed. We see an open suitcase—packed full, with the exception of socks.*)

MARY. You want to bring your brown socks or your blue socks?

(*BILL does not answer, engrossed in his TV.*)

MARY. Bill, do you want to bring your brown socks or your blue socks?

BILL. Blue.

(*MARY packs blue socks. The others are put away in a dresser.*)

MARY. You'll have to carry the suitcase to the car.

(*BILL does not respond. MARY lifts the suitcase. It is too heavy.*)

MARY. Oh, I forgot to tell you. Margaret and Jack are splitting up. Did you hear me?

BILL. Blue!

MARY. That suitcase is too heavy for me. What are you watching?

BILL. "Back to Bataan." Ssh.

MARY. Nobody's talking. They're just shooting at each other.

BILL. Mary, do you see me watching my movie? Do I interrupt you when you watch "Dynasty?"

MARY. No, you just go out.

BILL. Then go out. You have to take the suitcase to the car anyway.

MARY. When am I supposed to talk to you?

(*BILL does not answer. MARY tries lifting the suitcase*

again, but can't.)

MARY. Tomorrow's our anniversary. Do you think we might talk to each other tomorrow? It is a special occasion.

BILL. Thirty years.

MARY. Twenty-nine years.

BILL. Same thing.

MARY. Remember when you used to be romantic? When we were first married I thought you were the most romantic man in the world. What happened to you?

(*BILL rises in his sloppy bathrobe and Marine hat.*)

BILL. What are you talking about? I'm still romantic.

MARY. When is the last time you took me to a movie? We used to go out all the time.

BILL. We just saw "Death Wish 2" didn't we?

MARY. When's the last time you took me to a movie *I* wanted to see? I wanted to see "On Golden Pond" and now it's gone.

BILL. I told you to go see that during the day when I'm working.

MARY. Did you ever think for a minute to do something for me?

BILL. What's gotten into you? Have you been reading "Cosmo" again? I told you I don't want that junk in my house.

MARY. You go to work. You come home. We eat. We watch television. And we go to bed. We never do anything together anymore.

BILL. We eat together, don't we? We watch TV together, don't we? When I saw "Death Wish 2," who'd I ask to go with me? You.

MARY. Who says chivalry is dead? You're a regular Don Juan, aren't you?

BILL. You want to go see "On Golden Pond?" We'll go see "On Golden Pond."

MARY. It's gone now.

BILL. Good. I didn't want to see that anyway. Now let me watch my movie.

MARY. Why did you invite the kids for the weekend? I wanted to spend a nice quiet weekend all alone with you.

BILL. What for? We're alone all the time. Except for when the kids need money. Or your daughter has a fight with that bum she's married to. I thought it would be a nice surprise.

MARY. I thought we could relive our honeymoon. I wanted to make everything the same as it was.

BILL. Have you looked at us lately? Nothing is the same as it was.

MARY. Would you carry this to the car for me? Please?

BILL. As soon as the commercial comes on. Ssh.

MARY. You might as well talk to yourself around here.

BILL. You're starting to act like your mother, Mary. Do you know that?

MARY. I am not. Don't you ever say that.

BILL. You never stop talking. You never let me watch my war movies without talking. That's how your father died, you know. He was talked to death.

MARY. You are always watching those stinking war movies. When am I ever supposed to talk to you?

BILL. During commercials. When you see John Houseman, take it as your cue.

MARY. We're never getting cable! You hear me? Never! (*MARY turns the volume down.*) Can I talk now? Commercial's on.

BILL. Of course you can talk.

MARY. Margaret and Jack broke up. ARE YOU LISTENING TO ME?

BILL. Of course I'm listening to you. When did this happen?

MARY. He's leaving her for a nineteen year old college girl.

BILL. Yeah? Good for him.

MARY. Bill. Margaret is so upset. She said she never even saw it coming.

BILL. That's what she gets for gaining all that weight. Maybe next time she'll take better care of herself.

(MARY looks down at herself and tries fixing herself up.)

MARY. I've been exercising again. Have you noticed any difference yet?

BILL. Yeah, I think your head got smaller.

MARY. Bill? Be honest with me . . . have you ever thought about nineteen year old college girls?

BILL. Constantly. But what do I need them for? I've got the best girl in the whole world right here. I don't need any sexy, young, attractive girls. I've got you.

MARY. Thank you.

BILL. I don't need anyone or anything. I've got it all in one woman. Twenty-nine of the best years a man could ever hope for.

MARY. That's it? No insult?

BILL. What do you mean?

MARY. Aren't you going to insult me? You can never just compliment me. You always have to insult me. Either I'm too fat or I'm too old or I talk too much.

BILL. What's the matter with you?

MARY. Go ahead. Insult me.

BILL. I don't want to insult you.

MARY. You've been doing it all day.

BILL. I have not. I'm trying to watch a war movie. "Guadalcanal Diary."

MARY. (*correcting him*) "Back to Bataan." You've seen it thirty times. Why don't you stand next to the screen and do the lines along with the actors?

BILL. These films are about the most interesting chapters of American history. Sit here and learn something.

MARY. Do you have an extra hat for me to wear?

BILL. Hey. Don't you make fun of my hat. I served this country with this hat. I even won you with this hat. You remember?

MARY. Of course I remember.

BILL. This is my lucky hat. I got you. And we won the war.

(*THEY kiss.*)

MARY. Things haven't changed that much in thirty years.

BILL. Twenty-nine years.

MARY. Same thing.

(*THEY kiss. BILL stops her.*)

BILL. Movie's back on. (*BILL pushes MARY aside to get to the TV and turn up the volume.*)

MARY. You're a regular Don Juan. You want me to put

lipstick on the screen and you can have a real good time?

BILL. What?

MARY. Why do I stay with you? Why? If I had any sense I'd go out and have an affair.

BILL. Who'd have you, Mary?

MARY. A lot of people. Maybe.

BILL. You have to admit. I'm better than nothing.

MARY. There you have me.

BILL. Let me fill you in on something. Every other guy my age has had affairs left and right. Cheated on their wives. Deceived their wives. Lied to their wives. Not me. I've spent every night with you since we've been married. Twenty-nine years and we haven't been apart one single night. No affairs. No cheating. No deceiving. And no lies.

MARY. And no romance. I want to have fun.

BILL. We have fun.

MARY. Folding socks and watching you watch old war movies is no fun.

BILL. It's fun for me. You make it sound like we don't do anything at all.

MARY. Tell me what we do? Tell me what we do do.

BILL. Tell me what we do-do? We go to the movies once a week, don't we? We go out to dinner a couple of times a week, don't we?

MARY. I want to do something out of the ordinary. Like we did when we were younger. I want to do something wild.

BILL. You want to do something wild? Go run around the block in your underpants. Go ahead. You better hurry. You're losing the light.

MARY. Everything we do is routine.

BILL. We go on vacation every year.

MARY. To the islands. So you can play more golf. And

it's only one week a year. That's not fun. That's routine.

BILL. One week vacation is enough. I'm too old for fun, now. I just want comfort. I want to be comfortable. I'm comfortable with you and I'm comfortable in my bathrobe watching my war movies. You better get going, the sun goes down in an hour.

MARY. When we were first married, we used to go for long walks under the stars.

BILL. I have corns. You want to see me limping?

MARY. There's no talking to you.

BILL. Now you're getting the idea. When I'm watching TV, there's "no talking" to me.

MARY. Are you really "comfortable" with me? I mean, really "content?"

BILL. Yes, of course I am.

MARY. And you love me?

BILL. Mary. You know I love you.

MARY. Then make me happy.

BILL. Mary, it's daylight.

MARY. I'm unhappy, Bill.

BILL. You are not unhappy. You are happy. I'm happy. Everybody's happy. We're both happy!

MARY. I am not happy. I'm fifty-two years old. I'm overweight. And I'm getting wrinkles. And I want to do something wild.

BILL. You want to do something wild? Make stuffing AND mashed potatoes for dinner tomorrow.

MARY. I'm trying to hang on to my youth and you aren't helping at all.

BILL. I care. You know I care. You're going through a phase right now. That's all it is. There's a word for it. Menopause.

MARY. Thank you. That was seven years ago.

BILL. What would you like to do? What kind of fun are we talking about?

MARY. I know . . . when we go away for the weekend . . . make love to me outdoors.

BILL. What? Are you crazy?

MARY. We can sneak out at night and meet under the old sycamore tree and we can make love under the stars.

BILL. Oh, that'll be cute. That'll be real cute. Two fat naked old people rolling around under a rotted tree. What if the kids see us?

MARY. Go watch your movie. I won't bother you. (*MARY tries dragging the suitcase out the door.*)

BILL. I'll take that down in a minute. It's just about over, anyway.

MARY. I can carry it.

BILL. You want to go to a movie tonight?

(*MARY stops, hopeful.*)

MARY. What's playing?

BILL. "Firefox." Clint Eastwood.

MARY. I'll go get ready. (*MARY lugs her suitcase out as BILL continues watching his movie.*)

BLACKOUT

Scene Four

(*LIGHTS UP on DANNY in his suburban bedroom. HE is packing for a weekend in the country. HE calls off to someone.*)

DANNY. I'm up here! Come on up!
PAUL. (*off*) Are you alone?
DANNY. Come on in.

(*PAUL sheepishly enters the room.*)

PAUL. Where's Jennifer?
DANNY. She's at Pathmark, buying me Yodels.
PAUL. What are you doing?
DANNY. What does it look like I'm doing?
PAUL. (*gleeful*) You're leaving Jennifer?
DANNY. I'm packing.
PAUL. I can see that you're packing. Going away for a business trip?
DANNY. Going away for the weekend.
PAUL. Alone?
DANNY. Together. With Jennifer. Who do you think I'm going away with?
PAUL. "Poot." I thought you might be meeting your girlfriend somewhere. Your "Mystery Mistress."
DANNY. I'd rather not talk about her.
PAUL. Why?
DANNY. It's all over with.
PAUL. What?
DANNY. I ended it. I ended the affair.
PAUL. Why? What would you want to go and do that for?
DANNY. I don't want to talk about it.
PAUL. Danny! The best thing for your marriage is an affair. It makes you appreciate your wife more because you have a better chance of losing her. Listen to me, we've been best friends for fifteen years. I think you're making a mistake.

DANNY. Well, don't tell me that now. It's too late now. I'm going to make up to Jennifer. (*DANNY begins crossing to the dresser. PAUL grabs him.*)

PAUL. Why? Why would you want to do that?

DANNY. She's my wife. That's why. I've neglected her for too long. (*DANNY starts to cross away again. PAUL grabs his arm.*)

PAUL. No, you haven't.

DANNY. This affair opened my eyes. (*DANNY tries to walk away and PAUL again grabs his arm.*)

PAUL. No, it didn't.

DANNY. Look what I bought her. (*DANNY crosses to the dresser. PAUL, a beat late, grabs and misses him.*) (*DANNY opens the dresser and pulls out a bottle of Charlie.*)

PAUL. Charlie.

DANNY. It's her favorite.

PAUL. I'm sure she'll love it. But it's an awfully small bottle. You should get the big economy size.

DANNY. You think so?

PAUL. Buddy . . . think about what you're doing. You cheated on your wife for one and a half years. You think she doesn't know? She knows.

DANNY. She trusts me. She doesn't know. (*DANNY resumes packing.*)

PAUL. Ah, I'll bet she's cheated on you, too.

DANNY. Jennifer? (*laughs*) Jennifer? Cheat on me? (*laughs*) That's a hot one.

(*PAUL joins in the laughter.*)

PAUL. Why not? You cheat. Why shouldn't she cheat?

DANNY. I'd kill her. That's why. And the guy. I'd kill

him worse.

(*PAUL stops laughing.*)

PAUL. Now that you mention it, she doesn't seem the type.

DANNY. If there's one person in this world I know I can trust, it's Jennifer. Besides, if she ever found out. It would kill her. So you better keep your blabbermouth shut.

PAUL. (*seating DANNY*) Exactly what I'm leading up to. You just made the other woman angry by breaking up with her. Right?

DANNY. Right.

PAUL. She feels used, cheap, vile, low . . . dirty. She has only one alternative. Revenge! She'll tell Jennifer everything. You want Jennifer to know everything, Danny?

DANNY. Of course not.

PAUL. Then call up your friend and make up with her. (*PAUL hands DANNY the receiver.*)

DANNY. (*rising*) She wouldn't do something stupid like that.

PAUL. (*pushing him back down*) Yes she would!

DANNY. (*rising*) You don't even know her.

PAUL. (*pushing him back down*) I know her type. (*PAUL sits, with phone in lap.*) Listen to me, I've been fooling around with married women for years. Believe me, call her and make up before it's too late.

DANNY. (*hanging up phone – on PAUL'S hand*) I can't. (*DANNY rises and paces as PAUL winces in pain.*) It was wrong. I never should have cheated.

PAUL. Why do you want to end this affair? You always talk about how special she is.

DANNY. I do? Yes, that's true.

PAUL. And how great she makes you feel?

DANNY. That's true.

PAUL. And how great she is in bed?

DANNY. That's true.

PAUL. And how you wished you married her instead of Jennifer.

DANNY. That's not true. I never said that.

PAUL. You inferred it.

DANNY. I never did.

PAUL. You thought it.

DANNY. That's a lie.

PAUL. Did you ever say. "I'm glad I never married Whats-Er-Name?" What is her name, anyway?

DANNY. None of your business. That's her name.

PAUL. Who is this "Poot-Girl?" If it's over with, you can tell me.

DANNY. I can never tell anyone.

PAUL. I'm your best friend. Trust me.

DANNY. Just think of her as a "chippy."

PAUL. "Chippy?"

DANNY. Tramp.

PAUL. Why should I think of her as that?

DANNY. Because I found something out about her. That's why.

PAUL. What? What did you find out?

DANNY. (with hesitation) She's seeing another guy.

(PAUL laughs openly in DANNY's face.)

PAUL. She's seeing another guy? That's it? (laughs)

DANNY. You sound like her.

PAUL. You broke up with her because she's seeing

another guy?

DANNY. Don't you understand? I almost gave up my marriage for her. I was all set to get a divorce for her and now she's seeing another guy.

PAUL. That chippy!

DANNY. That tramp! I almost lost Jennifer and it's all your fault.

PAUL. What do you know? I mean, what do you mean? Who is this girl? Why won't you tell me her name?

DANNY. Because I'm ashamed.

PAUL. Why? Is she a hooker or something?

DANNY. Something like that.

PAUL. No wonder you're ashamed. (*reclining on the bed*) I went out with a hooker once. I didn't know she was one at the time. I just figured I was doing good with her, you know?

DANNY. When did you find out she was a hooker?

PAUL. Two weeks later. On my birthday.

DANNY. What did she give you?

PAUL. Gonorrhea.

DANNY. You had VD? Get off of my bed!!

PAUL. I'm cured now.

DANNY. Get off of my bed!!!

PAUL. I'm cured now!!

DANNY. (*wiping bedspread off*) Are you sure? I'm not lending you my tennis racket until you wash your hands.

PAUL. Where is it?

DANNY. In the closet.

(*PAUL starts for the closet. DANNY stops him.*)

DANNY. I'll get it. I don't want you touching my doorknobs. (*DANNY fishes in the closet.*)

PAUL. I'm going away for a real romantic weekend. With a real sexy lady.

DANNY. Yeah? Anyone I know?

PAUL. I wish.

DANNY. Who is she? A new one? Or someone I've met?

PAUL. A new one. I don't think you know her. I went to college with her.

DANNY. Who is she?

PAUL. Oh no. You have your mystery girlfriend. I have mine.

DANNY. Since when?

PAUL. Since now. She's blonde. That much I'll tell you. Just like your mistress.

DANNY. Ex-mistress.

PAUL. Yeah. We've always had the same taste in women.

DANNY. Why did she have to do this to me?

PAUL. I can't tell you how sorry I am things turned out like this.

DANNY. Thanks. You're a real pal, Paul. Where are you going with your date?

PAUL. I don't know. She called and told me to pack for an intimate weekend in the country.

DANNY. You dog. That's my kind of girl. Poot used to do stuff like that all the time. Of course I could never go, but it's the thought that counts.

PAUL. You keep the thoughts, I'll take the weekend. Where are you two going?

DANNY. Jennifer's folks are celebrating their hundred and fiftieth anniversary. We have to go help them blow out the candles.

PAUL. She's very romantic. I won't even know where we are going until we get there. It's going to be a surprise. I hope it's somewhere secluded.

DANNY. Boy, I envy you. I have to spend the weekend with the Great Santini. You never met Jennifer's father, did you?

PAUL. No, I never met any of her family.

DANNY. He loves the smell of napalm in the morning.

PAUL. Well, I'll be thinking of you.

DANNY. I wish we could trade places.

PAUL. Me too. Thanks for the racket. Give Jennifer a kiss for me.

DANNY. I will. Have fun.

(*THEY shake hands. PAUL starts to exit, with the racket. DANNY looks at his own hand and calls.*)

DANNY. Oh, Paul?

(*PAUL stops and turns back.*)

DANNY. Try not to touch anything on your way out.

PAUL. I'm cured now!!!

BLACKOUT

Scene Five

(*LIGHTS UP on KATHY's apartment, where we see her packing the corset DANNY gave her into a suitcase. The DOORBELL rings. KATHY quickly closes the suitcase and slides it under the bed. SHE answers the door, and we see JENNIFER – out of breath and obviously distraught.*)

JENNIFER. Kathy? Can I come in?

KATHY. Jennifer? What are you doing here?

JENNIFER. I was out for a walk and I happened to be passing by.

KATHY. You live twelve miles away.

JENNIFER. I know. My feet are killing me. Can I sit down?

KATHY. Are you all right?

JENNIFER. Yes.

KATHY. What's wrong?

JENNIFER. Nothing. Not a thing.

KATHY. You're sure?

JENNIFER. Yes.

KATHY. How's Danny?

JENNIFER. He's fine.

KATHY. How are you and he getting along?

JENNIFER. Why do you ask?

KATHY. No reason. I was just wondering.

JENNIFER. Great. Terrific. Never better. (*A quick whimper escapes.*)

KATHY. Jennifer, what's wrong?

JENNIFER. Nothing. Not a thing.

KATHY. Don't tell me nothing. You walked twelve miles over here and nothing's wrong?

JENNIFER. Oh! (*The dam breaks and a siren-cry escapes.*)

KATHY. Jennifer! Why are you crying?

JENNIFER. I did something terrible. (*SHE wails.*)

KATHY. Did you bounce another cheque?

JENNIFER. Worse. (*SHE wails.*)

KATHY. You scraped your car on the divider again?

JENNIFER. Worse. (*SHE wails.*)

KATHY. You lost your credit cards?

JENNIFER. Worse! I cheated!

KATHY. At what? One of those supermarket contests?

JENNIFER. No! I *cheated*.

KATHY. I don't get it. You cheated at Bingo?

JENNIFER. No. With another man.

KATHY. With another man?

JENNIFER. Bingo!

KATHY. You!? (*KATHY laughs uncontrollably.*)

JENNIFER. It's not funny.

KATHY. Oh yes it is. More than you know. When did this happen?

JENNIFER. Last week.

KATHY. With whom?

JENNIFER. One of Danny's best friends.

KATHY. Oh, Jenny, couldn't you have cheated with a stranger?

JENNIFER. What for?

KATHY. If all you wanted was sex . . .

JENNIFER. I didn't want sex. I wanted him.

KATHY. Who is it?

JENNIFER. You never met him. (*crying*) I'm so ashamed.

KATHY. What are you going to do?

JENNIFER. What do you think I'm going to do?

KATHY. There's only one thing TO do.

JENNIFER. I'm going to confession.

KATHY. You've got to tell Danny.

JENNIFER. I couldn't. He'd leave me.

KATHY. I know. I mean, he would not.

JENNIFER. You don't know Danny like I do. You wouldn't think it to look at him, but he's very old-fashioned. He'd never forgive me.

KATHY. I'd think it to look at him.

JENNIFER. I feel so awful.

KATHY. Why? Because you cheated?

JENNIFER. No. Because I want to cheat again. I liked it!

KATHY. Who is this guy?

JENNIFER. He makes me feel so special. Like a real woman. Like I'm a princess. Like I'm a prize.

KATHY. What about Danny?

JENNIFER. He makes me rotate his tires. (*wails*)

KATHY. Now what's wrong?

JENNIFER. I don't want to get caught.

KATHY. Nobody wants to get caught, Jennifer. How could you possibly get caught?

JENNIFER. I might squeal on myself. I'm terrible at keeping secrets. Oh, I've got to get home. It's getting late and I forgot to mow the lawn. I don't want to make Danny suspicious.

KATHY. Take the bus. I'll see you tomorrow. In the country. I can't wait for you to meet my new guy. You'll love him.

JENNIFER. Who is it?

KATHY. A guy I went to college with. I ran into him a couple of weeks ago. We've been seeing each other off and on.

JENNIFER. Oh, Kathy, I'm glad. You haven't dated in so long, Mommy thought there was something wrong with you.

KATHY. I got tired of being celibate.

JENNIFER. Kathy. Don't be disgusting. Is he a nice guy?

KATHY. Yes. He's a nice guy.

JENNIFER. He must be if he agreed to spend a boring weekend with Mommy and Daddy.

KATHY. Well, he didn't exactly.

JENNIFER. What do you mean, "He didn't exactly?"

KATHY. He kind of thinks he's spending an intimate romantic weekend all alone with me.

JENNIFER. Why does he think that?

KATHY. Because I told him that. How else could I get him to come? Daddy isn't going to let us sleep together.

JENNIFER. He still gives Danny and me a hard time.

KATHY. So, I told him it would just be him and me and a weekend he'll never forget.

JENNIFER. What's his name?

KATHY. I'm not telling you anything about him. None of you. Until you meet him. That way Daddy won't give him a hard time for being unemployed.

JENNIFER. He's out of work?

KATHY. I shouldn't have said anything.

JENNIFER. I won't tell Daddy. What kind of work is he out of?

KATHY. I'm not quite sure. He won't talk about it. He's ashamed at making me pick up the bill all the time.

JENNIFER. You pay for him?

KATHY. I don't mind.

JENNIFER. He lets you?

KATHY. I told you he was ashamed.

JENNIFER. Don't sell yourself so cheap, Kathy. Hold out until the right guy comes along.

KATHY. I held out for two years. I'm not good at holding out.

JENNIFER. You've gotten every guy you've ever wanted.

KATHY. Almost every guy. Trust me, Jennifer. You'll like him. You'd go for him yourself.

JENNIFER. (*checking watch*) I've got to go. If the hedges aren't clipped, he'll know something's up. Thanks for listening to me. You're a great sister.

KATHY. Yeah well . . . I'm not that great.

JENNIFER. If you ever need anything, you call me, too. Money, advice, anything. Everything I have is yours if you want it.

KATHY. I'll keep that in mind. Give Danny a kiss for me.

JENNIFER. I will. Oh, I feel so much better now. This will be fun. I bet it's a terrific weekend. I got them a Mr. Coffee. What did you get them?

KATHY. There was a book on Hitler I was going to get Daddy, but I figured he already had it. I'll pick something up on the way.

JENNIFER. I can't wait to meet your new boyfriend.

KATHY. I can't wait to see your reaction. And Danny's too.

JENNIFER. I'm glad we can all be together. I bet this is one anniversary Mommy and Daddy will never forget!

CURTAIN

ACT TWO

Scene One

(*CURTAIN RISES on a country home. It is rustic. We
see woods out the picture window. The front door is
U.S.R. and two other exits D.L. and D.R. lead off
to the kitchen-dining room area and the bedrooms.
MARY is seen dusting the coffee table, dressed
beautifully for this special occasion. SHE rearranges
the flower arrangement and repositions a greeting
card. From the kitchen enters BILL, dressed in T-
shirt and work pants. And Marine hat. HE eats a
sandwich, spilling crumbs everywhere.*)

MARY. Bill, go put a tie on.

BILL. I'm eating.

MARY. The kids will be here any minute. Please, go put
a tie on. For me.

BILL. Put a tie on? For that bum your daughter's married to?

MARY. No. Put a tie on for me.

BILL. Can I eat my sandwich first?

MARY. We're eating in half an hour!

BILL. I'm hungry now.

MARY. Did you see the flowers Kathy sent us? (*reading
from card*) "Happy Anniversary to Mom and Dad."

BILL. Who are those people on the front of the card?

MARY. I don't know who they are.

BILL. It's like we're getting the card from those people.

MARY. They're models.

BILL. It's a nice card. Very thoughtful.

MARY. Isn't it?

BILL. Too bad those people are on the front. What did Jennifer and the bum send us?

MARY. I guess it hasn't been delivered yet.

BILL. Yeah. You know why it hasn't been delivered yet? 'Cause there's nothing to deliver. That cheap bum. Why did she marry him, anyway?

MARY. She was in love with him.

BILL. I kept saying to myself, "Please let her be pregnant. Please let her be pregnant." All through the wedding I kept saying that.

MARY. Why did you say that?

BILL. I wanted there to be an excuse. If she married him because she actually wanted to, she's as much a loser as he is.

MARY. You're making crumbs! Why don't you go eat over the sink?

BILL. Why don't I just go stand outside?

MARY. I just cleaned up in here. Go put a tie on.

BILL. Why do I have to wear a tie? Is the bum going to wear a tie? He probably doesn't even wear one to work.

MARY. He's a writer, Bill. Why would he wear a tie to sit in front of a typewriter? Nobody would see him.

BILL. See that? Did you hear what you just said? That's what's wrong with these kids today. Just 'cause nobody sees them, they don't wear ties.

MARY. Oh, so that's what's wrong with them.

BILL. They have no sense of pride today. When I was

their age, I wouldn't go anywhere unless I looked my best.

MARY. I'm glad to see you've maintained such high standards. Go put a tie on. So I can choke you with it.

BILL. I'm going.

MARY. And don't make crumbs.

BILL. I'll leave a path so you can find me.

MARY. We don't have time. The kids will be here any minute.

BILL. We don't have time for what?

(MARY flirts with him. It goes right over his head.)

MARY. It is our anniversary . . .

BILL. Mary, calm down. There's nothing as pathetic as a horny old lady.

MARY. I'm not old. Don't you ever call me that again.

BILL. I've got a surprise for you later.

MARY. What? You're going to act nice to me?

BILL. No. I have something up my sleeve.

MARY. Probably crumbs.

BILL. A little anniversary surprise.

MARY. You got me a present? On your own?

BILL. As a matter of fact, I did.

MARY. When did you learn how to do that?

BILL. I took courses.

MARY. You want to open them now or wait?

BILL. Let's wait. The kids will be here any minute. Let's wait until they go to bed.

MARY. I've been meaning to ask you about that. Kathy's bringing a boy . . .

BILL. No.

MARY. No what?

BILL. No way. They're not sleeping together.

MARY. She's almost thirty years old.
BILL. In my house . . .

(*MARY mimics him behind his back.*)

BILL. . . . they live by my rules. I am the king of this castle. I don't believe in sex before marriage and they know that.
MARY. We did it.
BILL. That was different. I *married* you, didn't I?
MARY. It was close.
BILL. It won't kill them to use blankets to keep warm. Besides, what if I want to use the bathroom in the middle of the night? I'd have to pass her room and God knows what noises I'd hear coming out of there. I'd never be able to get back to sleep.
MARY. So, I'm sure we can find something to do all night.
BILL. Yeah. Bang on the wall.

(*DOORBELL*)

MARY. (*running back and forth*) They're here! Go put a tie on! Hurry up! They're here!
BILL. All right. "They're here!" Don't wet your pants, Mary. (*BILL exits to the bedrooms. MARY wipes crumbs from the coffee table and primps before answering the door. At the door is JENNIFER – alone. SHE carries a wrapped Mr. Coffee box. THEY hug and kiss.*)
JENNIFER. Hi Mom.
MARY. Baby.
JENNIFER. You look so pretty. (*JENNIFER enters the room and sets down the present. MARY looks out the door.*)

MARY. Where's Danny?

JENNIFER. Who?

MARY. Your husband.

JENNIFER. Oh, him. He's outside. Getting the suitcases and swearing.

MARY. Did you have another fight? Don't tell me you had another fight.

JENNIFER. No. It's the same old fight. It never ends. (*THEY hug.*) Happy anniversary. Where's Daddy?

MARY. He's getting dressed up.

JENNIFER. Daddy? Dressed up?

MARY. (*heading for her present*) He doesn't go anywhere unless he looks his best, you know. (*MARY shakes present to see what it is as BILL enters from bedrooms with the same T-shirt, work pants, Marine hat, and a tie.*)

BILL. Jenny. My little girl. Did you leave him yet?

JENNIFER. Happy anniversary, Daddy. You look . . . that's a nice tie.

BILL. Some people still wear them.

MARY. You look so distinguished.

BILL. Where's That Boy?

MARY. His name is Danny, Bill.

JENNIFER. Unloading the car.

BILL. You still together? You and That Boy?

MARY. His name is Danny, Bill.

JENNIFER. Six years.

BILL. Is he making you happy?

JENNIFER. Yes, Daddy. He takes good care of me.

BILL. Well, where is he?

JENNIFER. He's outside. He slammed his fingers in the car door and I told him not to come in until he stopped swearing.

BILL. He swears, huh? In front of you?
JENNIFER. Daddy, I want you to act nice to him today.
BILL. I'm nice to everybody.

(*DOORBELL*)

MARY. Answer the door, Bill.
BILL. I didn't hear anything.
MARY. Would you like a drink, Jennifer?
JENNIFER. Yes, some ginger ale, please.
MARY. Bill. Would you answer the door?
BILL. I already put a tie on, didn't I?
MARY. Bill. For me. Answer the door.
BILL. (*heading for the door*) Margaret made Jack answer the door, too.
JENNIFER. What is he saying now?
MARY. Don't listen to him.

(*BILL opens the door revealing DANNY, carrying a corsage box and a suitcase.*)

BILL. Nobody's there. (*BILL slams the door shut in DANNY's face.*)
MARY. Bill!
JENNIFER. Daddy!
BILL. That was a joke. Nobody can take a joke around here. (*BILL re-opens the door and DANNY staggers in. The corsage box is now smashed to bits.*)
DANNY. Happy anniversary, Sir.
BILL. Thank you. Come on in, boy. Come on in. Let me help you. You know my wife, don't you?
JENNIFER. Daddy.
DANNY. We stopped to get you a corsage, Mrs. H.

MARY. How nice.

BILL. We got a card from Kathy. Very thoughtful. With pictures of models on the front. Very nice.

(*MARY opens the smashed box and takes out a squashed corsage. Petals fall to the floor.*)

MARY. Isn't that lovely.

BILL. How long have you had that thing laying around?

JENNIFER. We just bought it, Daddy.

BILL. You got taken. It's all squashed.

(*DANNY shoots JENNIFER a look and heads straight for the bar.*)

MARY. It's very sweet. Would you care to pin it on me, Bill?

BILL. Allow me. (*BILL pins on the pitiful remains of a corsage.*)

MARY. I love corsages. Nobody buys them anymore. Every Mother's Day, we used to get one for my mother. She loved wearing them so much. People would say to her, "How beautiful." And she'd say, "My children bought it for me." She loved saying that.

JENNIFER. Well, now you can say that, too.

MARY. Who's going to see it?

BILL. Save it and wear it on Mother's Day.

MARY. It's not for eight months.

BILL. Believe me, it couldn't look any worse in eight months than it does right now. How's the writing business going, Danny? (*BILL shakes DANNY's hand. The one that was smashed in his car door.*)

DANNY. Great. My hand!!

BILL. You got a grip like a pansy.

JENNIFER. He just smashed his hand in the car door.

BILL. What are you working on now? Your last play bombed, didn't it?

DANNY. A play about Christopher Columbus. It's called "The World is Flat and That is That."

BILL. I had a great idea for a spy thriller. You know how those Japs are all over the place with their cameras clicking away at everything? Well, . . .

(MARY mimics the entire story word-for-word behind his back.)

BILL. . . . what if you found out that they were all spies and their cameras were responsible for the Japs taking over the world. With germ warfare. Don't you get it? You see, everytime they click a picture at you, they're actually shooting you with some kind of lethal bacteria that would, say, in ten years after they shot you, give you a deadly disease.

DANNY. Sounds great. *(downs his drink)*

BILL. I was thinking of writing it myself. I think anybody can write as long as they have a wife to support them.

MARY. Would you like some more wine, Danny?

DANNY. Thank you. Lots of it.

JENNIFER. Me, too. I'd like some more ginger ale.

MARY. *(at bar)* Don't drink too much. You'll ruin your appetites.

JENNIFER. What time is Kathy getting here?

MARY. She's late as usual. You tell her two or three and she shows up around seven or eight.

DANNY. No she doesn't. She's very punctual.

JENNIFER. We haven't seen her in three months, Danny.

DANNY. Oh. I thought I remembered that about her.

JENNIFER. I can't wait to meet her new boyfriend.

MARY. (*serving the drinks*) I hear he's very good-looking.

BILL. They're not sleeping together!

MARY. Bill.

DANNY. She's bringing him here? Today??

JENNIFER. Yes. I told you that. You never listen to me when I talk to you.

DANNY. She's bringing him here today?

JENNIFER. (*mocking his delivery*) Today. Yes. I told you that. (*sing-song*) She's bringing him here today.

BILL. What's wrong with that? We allow a lot of people here.

DANNY. Nothing. Not a thing. I haven't seen her with a boyfriend in so long, it's going to feel strange. May I have some more wine, please?

MARY. You haven't finished the wine in your glass yet.

DANNY. Oh. (*DANNY drains his glass and holds it out for more.*) No club soda, this time.

BILL. I told you about those writers. They drink like fish.

(*MARY is at the bar and the DOORBELL rings. DANNY leaps up, scaring MARY into spilling ice all over the place.*)

DANNY. NO ICE EITHER!

MARY. Bill, would you get the door?

BILL. I got the door last time. You get the door.

MARY. Here, Danny. Help yourself. (*MARY heads for*

the door as DANNY pours himself a drink, assisted by JENNIFER.)

BILL. I would've gotten it.

JENNIFER. Why are you drinking so much? Are you that nervous in front of my father?

DANNY. Good. Yes. That's it. I'm nervous in front of your father.

JENNIFER. Every family function, you get nervous.

(*DANNY and JENNIFER drink as KATHY is let in. SHE is dressed teasingly, for DANNY's sake. It does not go unnoticed.*)

KATHY. Happy anniversary, everybody.

MARY. Kathy! You're on time.

DANNY. And you're alone. (*to himself*) Oh, good.

JENNIFER. Well, where is he?

KATHY. (*smiling*) Oh, I knew there was something I forgot. Be right back. (*KATHY exits outside.*)

DANNY. Oh boy.

BILL. (*crossing with MARY to window*) Where's she going?

DANNY. Oh, boy.

MARY. Ssh.

KATHY. (*off*) This way. Watch your step.

BILL. What's she doing?

MARY. Ssh. It's her new boyfriend. We're going to surprise him.

BILL. (*gazing out*) What is he, disfigured?

MARY. That's a blindfold.

BILL. He looks like the Elephant Man.

PAUL. (*off*) Where are we, Kathy? I feel silly with this thing on.

DANNY. (*ears perking up*) That voice.

KATHY. (*off*) We're almost inside.

· PAUL. (*off*) I think I stepped in something.

KATHY. (*off*) Okay, get ready . . .

PAUL. (*entering*) Are we inside yet?

JENNIFER. No. It couldn't be.

(*DANNY and JENNIFER nervously drink.*)

KATHY. I'd like you to meet my family . . . (*takes off his blindfold*) . . . Paul.

(*DANNY AND JENNIFER spit their drinks all over BILL. Wide-eyed and speechless, PAUL takes in the room and its inhabitants.*)

BILL. Omigod.

PAUL. Omigod.

JENNIFER. Omigod.

DANNY. Holy shit!

BILL. (*wiping his wet shirt*) What's the matter with you two? Nice mouth on you.

PAUL. I'm sorry. I must have the wrong address. (*PAUL runs for the door, held back by KATHY.*)

KATHY. Paul, come back here.

DANNY. (*to BILL*) I'm sorry. I could never hold my liquor.

BILL. You can't even hold it in your mouth. Don't touch me.

KATHY. Paul, this is my family. Are you surprised?

PAUL. That's one word for it. I am definitely surprised. (*PAUL eyes JENNIFER. A rat caught in a trap. DANNY'S eyes glare at KATHY. JENNIFER'S glare at PAUL.)*

MARY. I'm Kathy's mother, Paul. How nice to meet you.

(PAUL's mouth opens and nothing comes out.)

KATHY. Don't be nervous, Paul. We don't bite.

PAUL. *(all HE can utter)* H-hi.

KATHY. I'd like you to meet my father, Paul. Daddy, this is Paul.

PAUL. H-hi.

BILL. I hear you're out of work.

*(PAUL looks at KATHY. SHE looks at JENNIFER, the
    OTHERS follow.)*

JENNIFER. I couldn't help it.

KATHY. That's my sister Jennifer and her husband, Danny.

PAUL. I know. *(angrily pulling KATHY aside)* I thought we were going to be all alone this weekend, Kathy. You really should have warned me.

DANNY. *(HE can't stand any more.)* What are you doing here?

PAUL. What are you doing here?

KATHY. *(innocent)* You know each other? How wild. How do you know each other?

DANNY. Oh, you might say we have similar interests.

(KATHY puts her arm around a nervous PAUL.)

KATHY. How funny.

PAUL. It's a scream. (*PAUL nervously laughs, but upon seeing JENNIFER's cold stare, HE stops short.*)

MARY. (*sitting*) How nice that you all know each other.

DANNY. Yes. We've known each other for years. Paul used to be my best friend.

JENNIFER. What do you know? I mean . . . what do you mean?

PAUL. What do you mean "used to be?" Mrs. Hogan, Mr. Hogan, Danny's a kidder. We're best buddies.

BILL. Strike one.

DANNY. (*glaring at KATHY*) In fact, we share everything we have. Isn't that right, Paul?

PAUL. Yeah? Why do you say that?

DANNY. I lent him my tennis racket for this weekend. I had no idea you were seeing Kathy, pal.

JENNIFER. Me either, pal . . . Paul. Kathy, you never told me your boyfriend's name. I wish you had so I would have known.

KATHY. Well, my mistake.

JENNIFER. No, my mistake.

PAUL. (*HE advances to explain to JENNIFER, but realizing where HE is, HE backs off.*) It's just a casual thing. Nothing serious. Just a dinner or two here and there. Nothing special.

BILL. Good. Then you won't mind sleeping out here on the couch.

(*MARY jabs BILL.*)

KATHY. (*for DANNY'S ears*) We've done more than just dinner here and there, Paul. I wouldn't say it's nothing special. We've gotten pretty serious over the past few weeks.

DANNY. Oh, you have, have you.

JENNIFER. (*at bar*) How interesting.

DANNY. (*advancing*) Exactly how close are we talking about?

MARY. (*rising*) I'd rather not hear about it, thank you. I'm so glad you're dating again, Kathy. We thought there was something wrong with you.

DANNY. (*noticing his upset wife by the bar*) What's wrong with you?

JENNIFER. Nothing. Not a thing.

BILL. What did you say to her now, Danny?

DANNY. Nothing. I didn't say anything to her. What's wrong with you, honey?

JENNIFER. Nothing. Not a thing. It's so nice that Kathy's dating again. I'm so happy for her.

KATHY. (*putting a loving hand on her shoulder*) Oh, Jen, how sweet.

JENNIFER. Get your hands off of me. (*JENNIFER runs off into the kitchen, crying like a siren.*)

MARY. It's so nice to have the family together. Isn't it, Bill?

KATHY. She hates to see me happy. Kiss me.

DANNY & PAUL. What?

KATHY. Kiss me . . . Paul.

PAUL. (*embarrassed and confused*) But your parents, I just . . .

KATHY. I said, kiss me, Paul.

PAUL. Yeah, but . . .

(*KATHY kisses him and HE is helpless in fighting her off. DANNY glares. BILL & MARY look to each other.*)

BILL. Yessir. It's nice to have the family together, all right.

(*DANNY's legs are shaking with anger. His drink shakes right out of his glass.*)

MARY. Let's go clean you up, Bill. Before your tie stains. I think they want to be alone.

BILL. All three of them? Help yourself to a drink, Danny. (*notices his drink spilling all over the floor*) On the house.

MARY. Dinner should be ready in about ten minutes, if someone wants to check it . . . Danny.

(*The kiss is still going strong.*)

DANNY. (*attempting to break it*) What line of work are you in, Paul?

(*PAUL waves him to go away and continues kissing. DANNY heads for the bar.*)

MARY. I guess this is just a romantic weekend. Romance is in the air. Kiss me, Bill.

BILL. You want my tie to stain, Mary?

(*MARY & BILL exit to the bedroom.*)

BILL. (*exiting*) How does he hold his breath that long?

PAUL. (*breaking the kiss*) Boy, I'm gonna like it around here. I can't get over the fact that we're all together.

DANNY. Well, get over it.

KATHY. I'll go give Jennifer a hand in the kitchen. Paul, why don't you go get the suitcases out of the car.

PAUL. You mean "suitcas*e*." I wish you told me we weren't going to be alone. (*embarrassed*) I didn't pack any clothes. Not one stitch.

DANNY. (*laughing*) You little devils. He didn't pack any clothes. Isn't that cute, Kathy? All he packed was my tennis racket.

KATHY. Your friend's an animal, Danny. He can't keep his hands off me.

PAUL. (*playing it big to throw DANNY off the Jennifer-Paul track*) What can I say? Kathy is the sexiest woman I've ever known. I dropped all of my other women for her, you know. All of them.

DANNY. You lucky guy, you. Did you happen to pack any clothes, Kathy?

KATHY. Yes, I packed clothes. Although I wish I didn't have to.

(*THEY kiss. DANNY burns.*)

PAUL. Isn't she something?

DANNY. Oh, she's something, all right.

PAUL. I'll go get the suitcase. But I don't have to wear the blindfold again, do I? (*PAUL laughs.*)

KATHY. No. But save it for later tonight.

(*PAUL laughs a big dirty laugh.*)

PAUL. Oh, what a woman. Aren't I a lucky bastard?

DANNY. You certainly are, Paul. You took the words right out of my mouth.

(*PAUL exits, laughing contentedly.*)

DANNY. YOU DIRTY BAST . . .

(*KATHY covers his mouth.*)

KATHY. Ssh.
DANNY. (*breaking free*) How dare you see him! How dare you bring him here.

(*KATHY begins laughing. A lot.*)

DANNY. My ex-best-friend. With my own tennis racket, too. What kind of a dirty joke is this to play on me? What are you laughing at? You think this is funny or something? This is not funny.
KATHY. Just one minute. I wasn't aware he was your best friend.
DANNY. How could you not know?
KATHY. Somehow your name hasn't popped up. Not everybody talks about you in this state.
DANNY. Says you.
KATHY. Besides, you left me to go back to your wife. You remember her? My sister? You are still married to her, aren't you?
DANNY. Leave her out of this. That has nothing to do with it. You did this on purpose just to see me squirm.
KATHY. How do you like it? That's what I've been going through for the past two years at every family function. Squirm, Danny. Squirm!
DANNY. Don't start, Kathy. This is worse and you know it.
KATHY. You're jealous.

DANNY. That has nothing to do with it.

KATHY. Have you spoken to Jennifer yet?

DANNY. No.

KATHY. Are you going to leave her for me or not?

DANNY. I can't.

KATHY. Very well, then. What I do from here on is my business.

DANNY. He's my best friend. You can't do this!

KATHY. I'm your wife's sister. That didn't stop you.

DANNY. You could've said no. Just remember that. You could've said no. You want to meet me later?

KATHY. No.

DANNY. I've missed you.

KATHY. How did you bowl last week?

DANNY. I didn't. The league's been cancelled since last May. I didn't even know it.

KATHY. What did you do on Monday night?

DANNY. I drove around your block for three hours with rented shoes on.

KATHY. I wasn't home.

DANNY. Where were you?

KATHY. What I do is my business.

DANNY. I hate this.

KATHY. So do I. Danny Boy.

DANNY. You know it drives me crazy when you call me Danny Boy.

(KATHY poses teasingly.)

KATHY. Does it? Danny Boy?

(DANNY reacts and is drawn to her.)

DANNY. All right. I'll talk to Jennifer. I'll talk to her.

KATHY. Oh, Danny.
DANNY. Oh, Poot.

(*THEY look to make sure the coast is clear and then THEY devour each other.*)

DANNY. (*breaking the kiss*) On one condition. You stop seeing him. That Benedict Arnold. That back-stabber.
KATHY. I promise.

(*THEY kiss.*)

DANNY. (*breaking the kiss, fast*) And no tennis. I don't want him near my racket.
KATHY. I promise. I'll talk him into taking my room and I'll sleep out here. Meet me tonight around midnight.
DANNY. Midnight. Right. I want you. Right here. Right now.
KATHY. And I want you. Not here. Not now.
DANNY. Midnight.
KATHY. So help me, I'll kiss you.
DANNY. So kiss me, I'll help you.
KATHY. You promise you'll talk to her?
DANNY. (*pausing*) Soon. I promise. (*DANNY goes to kiss her as THEY hear PAUL whistling as HE approaches the door. THEY fly apart. KATHY poses stiffly at couch and DANNY bee-lines to the bar when HE shoves a drink up to his lips as PAUL enters with the suitcase and the tennis racket.*)
PAUL. It's gonna be a full moon tonight. We should sneak out and fool around under the stars.
KATHY. (*putting her arms around him, extra-friendly*) Ooh. I'd love that.

DANNY. But . . . but . . but

KATHY. Where's your wife, Danny?

DANNY. Huh?

KATHY. Where's Jennifer?

DANNY. In the kitchen.

KATHY. Then go talk to her . . .

PAUL. Yeah, buddy, can't you see we want to be alone before her parents get back?

KATHY. He can't keep his hands off me.

DANNY. I think I will go see my wife. I can't keep my hands off her either.

PAUL. (*holding up the suitcase*) Where should I put this?

(*DANNY contemplates several choice answers.*)

DANNY. You wouldn't believe me if I told you.

KATHY. I'll be sleeping out here tonight, so just set it down. (*KATHY and PAUL tug of war the suitcase up and down.*)

PAUL. I'm sleeping out here. I wouldn't dream of taking your room away from you.

KATHY. Force yourself.

(*JENNIFER re-enters from the kitchen, composed and bent on making PAUL jealous. KATHY looks at DANNY who's ready to one-up her.*)

JENNIFER. Dinner's ready. Mom! Dinner's ready!

DANNY. I was just coming to help you. I missed you.

JENNIFER. You did? I missed you too.

(*THEY kiss. KATHY gets jealous.*)

KATHY. Kiss me, Paul.

PAUL. What?
KATHY. I said, kiss me.

(*THEY kiss. DANNY, who peeks at them, throws JENNIFER back in a dip, kissing her. KATHY, who peeks at them, throws PAUL back in a dip. A kiss-duel. From the bedroom, MARY enters.*)

MARY. Well, we didn't miss anything, Bill!

(*The kids break their kisses.*)

MARY. Did anything burn? In the kitchen?
JENNIFER. It's all ready.
KATHY. Where have you been, Mom?
MARY. We . . . wine is hard to get out of ties. Well, let's go in. Bill! Dinner's ready!

(*BILL enters in Marine hat, tie, and face covered with lip marks.*)

BILL. I'm starved. Everybody all set?
JENNIFER. We're all fine, Daddy.
BILL. Anything you need, Paul?
PAUL. Pajamas.
BILL. Beg your pardon.
PAUL. I didn't bring any pajamas.
BILL. Why not?
PAUL. I thought that . . . I forgot them.
MARY. Bill has an extra pair for you to wear.
BILL. I do not. I don't even know him.
MARY. We can wash them in the morning, Bill.
BILL. You don't have anything I can catch, do you?

DANNY. He's cured now.

BILL. What?

PAUL. That was a joke, sir. Danny's such a kidder.

MARY. Bill will be happy to lend you his pajamas, Paul.

BILL. Margaret made Jack lend out his pajamas, too.

KATHY. What's he saying now?

MARY. Don't listen to him. Well, shall we eat? Stuffing *and* mashed potatoes, Bill. Paul, you can sit between Kathy and me. You're part of the family now.

PAUL. If you don't mind, you all go ahead. I'd like to wash up. That suitcase was filthy.

KATHY. It is not filthy.

PAUL. Not any more. All the filth is on me . . .

MARY. It's the second door on the right around the corner.

PAUL. I'll be right in. I'm fast with my hands. Which one is it, again?

BILL. The room with the toilet in it. You can't miss it.

(MARY & BILL exit to the dining room.)

KATHY. Shall I wait for you, Paulie?

PAUL. No . . .

DANNY. Paulie?

PAUL. No, you go on in. I won't be but a minute.

(KATHY blows him a kiss and HE returns it reluctantly in front of JENNIFER. DANNY burns.)

KATHY. I'll keep your seat warm.

DANNY. I'll bet.

(KATHY exits to the dining room as PAUL tries signaling

*to JENNIFER. DANNY catches the end of it and
PAUL exits to the bathroom.*)

DANNY. (*extending his arm*) Well, darling? Shall we?
JENNIFER. What are you acting nice to me for? There's
nobody here.

(*DANNY looks around the room and sees that it is, in
fact, empty.*)

DANNY. (*dropping his arm*) Oh, I thought there were
people. (*DANNY heads for the dining room alone. HE
barks an order at JENNIFER.*) Get me a drink, will you?
White wine. (*DANNY exits.*)
JENNIFER. (*obeying*) Get it yourself. Oh. (*Looking off
towards the bedrooms, crying.*) That two-timer. That dirty
liar. (*SHE pours DANNY's white wine. SHE goes to pour
herself ginger ale, then changes her mind and pours a tall.
glass of scotch.*) Paul, why did you do this to me?

(*PAUL sneaks into the door frame. JENNIFER does
not see him.*)

PAUL. Psst. Psst.

(*JENNIFER looks up and to her left, but still
doesn't see him.*)

PAUL. Jennifer! Psst!
JENNIFER. (*holding drink out like a time-bomb*) Don't
you come near me.
PAUL. What are you doing, Jennifer. You don't drink.
JENNIFER. I'm drinking to forget you, Paul.

PAUL. Don't forget me. Let me explain.

JENNIFER. Don't you come near me.

PAUL. Let me explain.

JENNIFER. Don't you talk to me.

PAUL. Please, listen to me.

JENNIFER. Don't you touch me. I want to forget you, Paul.

PAUL. I can explain.

JENNIFER. You cannot possibly explain this one, Paul. I think all things considered, this is unexplainable.

PAUL. Would you believe me if I told you that I knew Kathy was your sister all along and used that as an excuse to see you here today?

JENNIFER. No.

PAUL. Really? I thought that was a good one. All right then . . . how about if I told you that I was attracted to her because she reminded me of you. She is your sister. That is possible. There is a similarity. I thought of you every time I was with her.

JENNIFER. Oh, come on, Paul. You can do better than that.

PAUL. No I can't. I didn't have any time to prepare this.

JENNIFER. You lied to me, Paul. You lied to me. You're lying to me now. You lied to me. (*JENNIFER gulps down her scotch.*)

PAUL. (*defeated*) But I didn't enjoy it. Do you think I enjoyed it?

JENNIFER. How many others are there? How many other married women have you suckered?

PAUL. Could you re-phrase that?

JENNIFER. No. How many other married women have you lured?

PAUL. Seven. Only seven.

JENNIFER. "Only seven?" "Only seven?" How can you possibly explain that?

PAUL. I'm fickle. It's different with you. I love you.

JENNIFER. Tell it to the marines.

PAUL. Keep your voice down before you do tell it to the Marine.

JENNIFER. You used me. You made me feel like I was special.

PAUL. You are special. She doesn't mean anything to me. I told you I was seeing other women, didn't I?

JENNIFER. She's my sister. How could you go with my own sister?

PAUL. She's not so bad, I like her.

JENNIFER. What?

PAUL. She's bad. Time-killer. That's all she is to me. A time-killer. Like all the other women I see. They're just time-killers until you're free to be with me. She doesn't mean a thing to me. I'm not even sure I like her. She's not very bright and she talks too much.

JENNIFER. Hey! That's my sister you're talking about!

PAUL. I'll make it up to you. I promise I'll stop seeing every woman I'm seeing if you'll forgive me. Every single one. Every married one, too. I don't want to lose you, Jennifer.

JENNIFER. You'd do that for me?

PAUL. I'm risking my own friendship with my best buddy for you, aren't I?

JENNIFER. You do love me, don't you?

PAUL. I'm sleeping out here tonight. Sneak out and meet me later. With the moonlight spilling in, it could be a very romantic rendezvous.

JENNIFER. (*tempted*) I don't know. Danny is a heavy sleeper. And we'd hear my father snoring, but . . . I can't.

PAUL. Sure you can.

JENNIFER. We'll get caught. I can't.

PAUL. How will we get caught? Danny's a heavy sleeper and your father snores. You just said so. What about your mother?

JENNIFER. She takes Valium.

PAUL. There you go. I'll give Kathy the brush and we're all set. Where's your sense of adventure?

JENNIFER. If you want adventure, go call my father a fag. I don't want adventure. I can't.

PAUL. Sure you can. I want you. Last week meant so much to me.

JENNIFER. Me too, Paul. More than you know. I hope you didn't mind it when we were making love and I called you Danny?

PAUL. (*Yes*) No. (*PAUL goes to kiss her and SHE stops him, hand in jaw. PAUL rubs his jaw in pain.*)

JENNIFER. Paul?

PAUL. What?

JENNIFER. Who's Mommy?

PAUL. What?

JENNIFER. When we were making love, you called me Mommy?

PAUL. . . . Commie. You must have heard me say Commie. I was dating a Russian girl. I love you.

JENNIFER. And you'll have me. Midnight. Out here. I'll give Danny some Nyquil and knock him out cold.

PAUL. That's what I love about you. You're so decisive.

(*THEY go to kiss. JENNIFER stops him again. More jaw business.*)

JENNIFER. Paul?

PAUL. What?

JENNIFER. Who's a better kisser?

PAUL. What??

JENNIFER. Who's a better kisser? Me or my sister?

PAUL. What are we talking . . . French or Regular?

JENNIFER. (*slapping at him*) Paul!

PAUL. You are! (*romantic*) You are.

JENNIFER. Oh, Paul!

(*THEY kiss. MARY enters from the kitchen to retrieve DANNY'S drink.*)

MARY. I'm sorry. Danny wanted his drink.

(*The kissing pair freezes as MARY walks past them and double-takes.*)

MARY. Boy, when they welcomed me to the family, I just got my ass pinched.

(*The couple flies apart. PAUL wipes lipstick off his mouth.*)

JENNIFER. Hi, Mom.

MARY. (*oblivious*) You'd better hurry. Your father's getting impatient.

JENNIFER. We're coming. I had to get Danny a drink.

MARY. I've got it right here. You just missed the boot camp story and the time your father met Ike.

JENNIFER. This isn't what it looks like, Mom.

MARY. Oh, now don't worry. I won't say a word. Your Uncle Dick welcomed me to the family in the very same way. Don't let her pinch your ass, Paul.

PAUL. Boy, am I famished. You know, Mrs. Hogan, I was just telling Jennifer that it's obvious where she and Kathy got all their beauty from.

(*JENNIFER and PAUL exit to the dining room.*)

JENNIFER. (*exiting to the dining room*) Going after the whole family now?

(*MARY looks out of the window.*)

MARY. It's going to be a full moon. I'll have to tell Bill.

BLACKOUT

ACT TWO

Scene Two

(*LIGHTS UP on the living room, around midnight. We see PAUL in pajamas much too small for him. HE pours two glasses of wine at the bar. KATHY enters from the bedrooms in a robe.*)

PAUL. (*sing-song*) Who is it?
KATHY. Kathy.
PAUL. (*spilling wine*) Oh shit.
KATHY. Who were you expecting?
PAUL. (*hiding bar*) Nobody.
KATHY. Then why did you pour two glasses of wine?
PAUL. I get very thirsty at night. What do you want?

KATHY. Nothing. I thought you were going to take my room.

PAUL. I know I said I would. But I can't. I can't take your bed away from you.

KATHY. Really, Paul. I can't let you sleep out here.

PAUL. I don't mind.

KATHY. The couch is so lumpy.

PAUL. I don't mind. I like lumps. (*sits on couch and bounces*) I'm a lump freak. I won't hear another word about it. You go back to bed.

KATHY. What time is it?

PAUL. Almost midnight.

KATHY. Oh shit.

PAUL. If you'll excuse me, I have to get my sleep. (*PAUL gives a big yawn and stretches.*)

KATHY. Then go take my room. You'll like it in there. It's a nice firm mattress. There's a gentle breeze coming in the window. And the moonlight spilling in will lull you right to sleep.

PAUL. I like lumps.

KATHY. Paul, you can't sleep out here.

PAUL. Why not?

KATHY. It's too noisy out here.

PAUL. Noisy? I haven't heard a thing since everybody went to bed.

KATHY. That's what I meant. It'll keep you up.

PAUL. I like noise.

KATHY. Then go take my room. You can hear my father snoring through the wall.

PAUL. I don't like that much noise. Why is it so important for you to sleep out here?

KATHY. Because I'm spoiled, Paul. I've always been spoiled. I get my way all the time or else I pout.

PAUL. That's true. You had your way with me.

KATHY. You wouldn't want to make me sleep in that room with my father snoring in the next room, would you? Would you Paul?

PAUL. Don't pout. I hate pouting.

KATHY. Thank you, Paul.

PAUL. But I hate the thought of sleeping in that bed more. Go pout.

KATHY. (*thinking quickly*) I know . . . it's very romantic outside, Paul. It could be very romantic . . . just you and me . . . and the stars . . . and this. (*KATHY opens her robe, revealing her corset. PAUL'S tongue hangs out.*)

PAUL. (*resisting*) That's a great idea . . . I . . . maybe . . . why don't you go outside and I'll meet you there.

KATHY. Why? What do you have to do?

PAUL. I have to brush my teeth.

KATHY. You just brushed your teeth.

PAUL. I forgot to floss.

KATHY. You don't need to floss. You go on out and I'll meet you under the sycamore tree.

PAUL. Why? What do you have to do?

KATHY. I have to take my pill.

PAUL. Oh. Right. All right. I'll go out. You go take your pill. Take your time. Drink a lot of water to be sure it goes down.

(*KATHY hands PAUL the blanket from the couch.*)

KATHY. Here. Find a nice quiet spot. I'll be as quick as I can.

PAUL. Okay, but take your time.

(*KATHY exits to the bedrooms, closing up her*

robe. PAUL waits for her to leave, then stomps heavily to the front door, slams it shut and steps back into the room.)

MARY. *(off)* Come on, Bill, I'll race you to the sycamore.

(PAUL panics and tries to find a place to hide. HE chooses the chair S.L. where HE sits and covers himself with the blanket, like a chair cover. BILL & MARY enter from the bedrooms. BILL wears his bathrobe and Marine hat and obviously nothing else. MARY wears a bathrobe and is bubbling with excitement. BILL is dying of embarrassment.)

BILL. If anybody sees us, Mary, I'll kill you.

MARY. Bill, this is the nicest anniversary present you could have given me. I thought those kids would never go to bed.

BILL. *(looking off into the kitchen)* Where's Kathy's boyfriend? What's his name?

MARY. Paul. His name is Paul. He must be in the bathroom.

BILL. Again? He must have a problem.

(PAUL sits up under the blanket.)

MARY. Hurry up, Bill. Let's go out and bask in the moonglow.

BILL. What, are you taking hormones or something?

MARY. This is the happiest night of my life. Outdoor sex!!

(PAUL pops his head out from the blanket, behind their

backs, with a look of shock and disgust.)

BILL. Ssh. Keep it down. I don't want an audience to gather out there.

MARY. Love under the stars!!

BILL. You sure you wouldn't rather have a toaster or something?

MARY. Bill, tonight I will be a woman fulfilled.

BILL. I'll give it my best shot, Mary.

MARY. I feel like a kid again. I feel young. I feel pretty.

BILL. I feel like a fool.

MARY. Not even you will ruin this night for me. Take some wine.

(*BILL goes to the bar, as PAUL disappears from view.*)

BILL. (*taking hold of the blanket*) Can't we take a blanket? What if I sit on some broken glass? Or a beetle? Or a field mouse?

MARY. No blankets. Just the grass beneath us. This is my present. You said "anything I wanted."

BILL. (*retrieving two glasses of wine at bar*) I know. But remember we still have to face each other in the morning. Let's not make horse's asses out of ourselves. (*BILL goes to sit on PAUL. MARY'S voice stops him.*)

MARY. I love you, Bill.

BILL. (*going to her*) I love you, Mary. Happy anniversary. I hope I still respect you in the morning.

(*THEY exit out the front door, first peeking left and
    right to make sure no one can see them. MARY turns
    out the lights as THEY go. THEY pass by the front
    window, peeking in to see if THEY are being no-*

*ticed. THEY exit out in the moonlight, as KATHY
enters in the darkness from the bedrooms. PAUL
lowers the blanket and calls off to her.*)

PAUL. Psst. Psst. (*whispered*) Over here.

(*THEY grope their way in the dark to each other. PAUL
smacks his shin on the coffee table.*)

PAUL. Ow . . . ow . . . ow . . . wow.
KATHY. (*whispered*) I love you.
PAUL. (*whispered*) I love you.

(*THEY kiss. KATHY breaks away.*)

KATHY. (*whispered*) What's wrong?
PAUL. (*whispered*) Nothing. Why?
KATHY. (*whispered*) You're kissing like Paul.
PAUL. (*normal voice*) I am Paul.
KATHY. Oh shit.
PAUL. Who are you?
KATHY. Kathy! (*flipping on the lights*) Naturally. Who
did you think I was?
PAUL. Nobody. You. I naturally assumed you were you.
But you returned so quickly.
KATHY. I swallow fast.
PAUL. Yeah well . . . I guess we should go outside
then. (*PAUL nervously looks over his shoulder.*)
KATHY. Yeah, well, I guess we should.

(*KATHY & PAUL exit out the front door, first looking
over their right shoulders towards the bedrooms, then
over their left shoulders. As THEY exit, PAUL steals*

*one last look over his right shoulder. THEY pass the
window outside, peeking in as THEY go by. As
THEY disappear from view, JENNIFER enters
from the bedrooms, dressed in a flannel nightgown
and robe. SHE nervously scans the room.)*

JENNIFER. Paul? Paul? Where are you?

*(PAUL appears at the window outside, hiding from
KATHY. HE sees JENNIFER and signals silently
for her to stay where SHE is. JENNIFER does not
see him and heads off towards the kitchen arch.)*

JENNIFER. Danny thinks I'm in the bathroom. He won't
fall asleep. Where are you?

*(PAUL disappears from the window. A split second later
JENNIFER exits into the kitchen-dining room area.
DANNY enters from the bedrooms in boxers, T-shirt,
robe, and socks. HE sneaks in expecting KATHY to
be waiting for him.)*

DANNY. *(whispered)* Kathy? Kathy? Where are you? It's
midnight. *(DANNY heads for the kitchen-dining room as
PAUL dashes in, expecting to embrace JENNIFER where
DANNY now stands. As DANNY checks his watch, PAUL
tries to make it back outside before being seen. DANNY
starts to turn around and in a moment of desperation,
PAUL flips the lights off.)*
DANNY. Who's that? Kathy?
PAUL. *(falsetto)* Mm-hm.

(DANNY heads for the voice and PAUL tries to sneak

by him towards the kitchen. DANNY grabs his arm
and stops him.)

DANNY. You little devil. I got here as soon as I could.
Jennifer's in the bathroom. I think she suspects
something. She tried to knock me out with Nyquil.
(DANNY puts his arms around "KATHY.") I missed you.
Kiss me, Poot. You smell good tonight. What is that,
Charlie?
PAUL. *(falsetto)* Mm-hm.
DANNY. Kiss me, Poot. *(no response)* Poot. Poot? . . .
Kathy?
PAUL. Paul.
DANNY. Oh shit.

(JENNIFER enters from the kitchen and flips the light
on. PAUL & DANNY stand frozen in their embrace,
DANNY'S hand on PAUL'S breast.)

JENNIFER. Omigod. What are you doing?
DANNY. Jennifer! This isn't what it looks like!

(Both men leap backwards.)

JENNIFER. What are you doing?
DANNY. This isn't what it looks like. Right Paul?
PAUL. *(lowering his register)* Right.
JENNIFER. What are you doing?
DANNY. Tell her, Paul.
PAUL. Right. He thought I was your sister.
DANNY. Wrong. *(DANNY winks furiously at PAUL.)*
No, I didn't.

PAUL. Yes you did. He thought I was your sister, Jennifer.

DANNY. (*winking desperately*) No, I didn't, Paul. *Pal.*

(*As DANNY'S gaze goes back and forth between PAUL & JENNIFER, PAUL tries miming to JENNIFER the truth — without DANNY seeing him.*)

DANNY. What a wild imagination he has. I thought he was you, Jennifer. That's good. Yeah. I saw you get out of bed and I came to find you.

JENNIFER. You're a lousy liar, Paul. Get away from my husband.

DANNY. Yeah, Paul. What's the matter with you?

(*From outside, we hear KATHY scream. SHE races in — minus bathrobe.*)

KATHY. (*Screaming as she races to DANNY'S side*) A bear! There's a bear outside! I saw a bear! Do something, Danny!

DANNY. Oh boy.

JENNIFER. What are you wearing? That's disgusting.

PAUL. (*grinning*) Hi, Poot.

DANNY. Jesus.

KATHY. Poot?

DANNY. Jesus.

KATHY. They know?

DANNY. Ch-rist.

JENNIFER. What are you wearing? That's disgusting. Only a pervert would buy something like that.

KATHY. Then your husband's a pervert.

JENNIFER. What?

DANNY. Jesus.

JENNIFER. You bought her that?

DANNY. It was on sale.

JENNIFER. You son of a bitch. Paul was telling the truth.

PAUL. Nobody ever listens to me.

DANNY. Now, wait a minute. I can explain.

JENNIFER. Go ahead. Explain.

DANNY. What?

JENNIFER. Explain. What do you have to say?

DANNY. . . . I have to go kill a bear. Let's go, Kathy.

(DANNY & KATHY try to make it outside. JENNIFER'S voice stops them.)

JENNIFER. Get over here. I'd like an explanation.

DANNY. Oh, you'd like an explanation! An explanation, you'd like. Oh. Uh . . . Paul will vouch for me. Go ahead, Paul. Start vouching.

PAUL. Danny and Kathy are having an affair.

DANNY. Thanks, pal.

PAUL. That's all right.

DANNY. There. You see now? Kathy and I are having an . . . nnNNOOOO!!!

KATHY. It's okay, Danny. Let's get it all out in the open.

JENNIFER. Get your hands off of my husband. He's mine! *(JENNIFER picks up DANNY by the throat. HE dangles in the air.)*

KATHY. Don't hurt anything!

JENNIFER. Have you been fooling around with my sister?

DANNY. I wouldn't say that.

PAUL. It's true.

DANNY. I know it's true, but I wouldn't say it.
JENNIFER. My own sister?
DANNY. She started it.
KATHY. That's a lie.
JENNIFER. How long has this been going on?
KATHY. A year and a half.
PAUL. Every Monday night.
JENNIFER. I thought that trophy was for bowling.
DANNY. Wait a minute! You're cutting off my wind.
JENNIFER. That's not all I'll cut off.
DANNY. What are you mad at me for? You shared the same bed when you were little, didn't you?

(JENNIFER knees DANNY in the groin.)

PAUL. So, you're Poot. What kind of a name is Poot?

(KATHY knees PAUL in the groin.)

JENNIFER. Don't you touch him. I'll tell you what kind of a name Poot is. It's short for "Puta."

(JENNIFER kicks DANNY in the backside and HE falls to the floor.)

KATHY. What's a "Puta," Danny?
PAUL. It means you're a Puta, Puta.
DANNY. You stay out of this. This has nothing to do with you.
PAUL. That's how much you know.
DANNY. This is all your fault, Paul. I'm never telling you anything ever again, you blabbermouth. You're a blabbermouth, Paul!

KATHY. What's left to tell?

PAUL. You'd be surprised.

JENNIFER. This is terrible.

PAUL. Terrible? This is terrific!

DANNY. You stay out of this, blabbermouth! This has nothing to do with you.

PAUL. Oh yeah? I've been fooling around with your wife, you moron!

DANNY. Oh, then that's different. (*rising up*) You what??

JENNIFER. Omigod.

KATHY. Omigod.

PAUL. What did I say?

JENNIFER. (*hitting PAUL*) Paul!

KATHY. Him?

PAUL. I couldn't help it, Jenny. I hate people that insist.

KATHY. (*laughs*) Him??

(*DANNY has found his tennis racket, which HE waves in the air like a battlesword.*)

DANNY. I'LLKILLYOUYOUSONOFABITCH!!! Stop laughing, Kathy.

(*DANNY waves the racket in the air as PAUL falls to his knees.*)

PAUL. Oh no! Not the tennis racket.

DANNY. I'm going to kill you, Paul. I'll serve your head all the way to Weehawken.

PAUL. Don't do it, Danny. I just finished paying for new caps.

(*DANNY breaks free of KATHY's hold and chases PAUL
      around.*)

DANNY. Do you have any last words?

PAUL. Don't I even get a cigarette first?

DANNY. No! Stand still so I can kill you, Paul.

PAUL. Why do you want to kill me? You were doing the
same thing.

DANNY. Not with my wife, I wasn't.

PAUL. Do something, Kathy.

KATHY. Kill him, Danny. He called me Puta.

PAUL. (*hiding behind JENNIFER*) Great. Do something, Jennifer!

JENNIFER. Danny . . . if you're going to kill someone,
kill me.

DANNY. You're next.

(*The chase continues. JENNIFER and PAUL make it to
      the bar, where THEY try to hide. KATHY holds back
      DANNY and his racket.*)

DANNY. You threw away our marriage for him? He's
a low-life! He had VD, you know.

KATHY. He did?

JENNIFER. (*slapping PAUL*) Omigod.

PAUL. I'm cured now!!

(*JENNIFER holds the ice bucket lid as a shield as SHE
      and PAUL pelt DANNY with ice. HE bats the cubes
      away with the racket as KATHY holds him back.
      PAUL holds the bucket in his free hand.*)

PAUL. Can't we discuss this like rational human beings?

DANNY. Of course we can. (*waving racket*) I'LLKILLYOUYOUSONOFABITCH!!

PAUL. That's much better. Help me, Jennifer. Our ammunition is melting.

JENNIFER. Danny . . . you're going to wake up Mommy.

PAUL. Oh, that's good, Jennifer.

DANNY. Why? Why?

KATHY. Who cares, Danny? Who cares? This is what we've waited to hear. It's your own fault you lost him, Jennifer. You could never make Danny happy. (*pushing up her bust*) I can make Danny happy.

(*PAUL and DANNY silently challenge the other to their side of the room, drawing lines for the other to cross, putting ice cubes on their shoulders for the other to try and knock off . . . etc. during the girls' verbal fight. THEY eventually give up and wait for the women to stop talking.*)

JENNIFER. You shut up. How could you do this, Kathy? My own sister. You always resented me marrying Danny.

KATHY. I was in love with him before you even knew him. I brought him over the house and you stole him.

JENNIFER. So what? You stole every boyfriend I ever had. You stole Scotty Wheeler and John Krahnert and Doug Deutsch . . .

KATHY. You got the one that counted.

PAUL. Girls . . . Danny . . . can't we reason this out? My arm is turning blue.

JENNIFER. You never made me happy, Danny.

DANNY. I bought you Charlie, didn't I?

JENNIFER. I never wore it, Danny.

DANNY. I'll kill you. Do you know how much that stuff costs? (*DANNY advances, KATHY still restraining him. PAUL and JENNIFER pelt them with cubes.*) Drop that ice bucket. Drop it. You want to knock my eye out?

(*PAUL nods.*)

PAUL. (*crying*) My arm is numb. I'm getting pains. Oh.

DANNY. Look at us. Look at us. A grown man chasing another grown man with a tennis racket. Have we come to this?

(*EVERYONE nods.*)

DANNY. This is crazy. (*calm*) Everyone just calm down. CALM DOWN!! I'm in control now. I'm in control. I'm calm. There. I think I can speak and act rationally now.

PAUL. Good. I have pains up to my shoulder now.

(*DANNY advances, calmly, to discuss this. PAUL tenses as HE nears.*)

DANNY. This is nobody's fault. It just happened.

PAUL. That's right.

DANNY. Now, I'm sorry, Jennifer, but Kathy makes me happy in ways that you never could.

KATHY. That's true.

DANNY. And I'm sure that Paul fills voids for you that I could never fill.

JENNIFER. That's true.

DANNY. As small as those voids may be. (*crosses away*) Now, we are not animals. We are humans. Reasoning, thinking, rational human beings. Let's put down these weapons of destruction. This racket. And those cubes. And reason this all out. Okay?

PAUL. Do you promise not to kill us?

DANNY. I promise. Drop it. Drop it.

(*PAUL studies DANNY and decides to set the ice bucket down. HE hands it to JENNIFER who sets it down. Lid on top. KATHY sighs with relief. DANNY raises his racket and advances.*)

DANNY. I'LLKILLYOUYOUBASTARDS! YOU CHEATERS!!

(*The chase resumes, out into the kitchen.*)

KATHY. (*off*) Don't do it, Danny!

PAUL. (*off*) Be careful with that thing!

(*OFF-STAGE SMASH*)

DANNY. (*off*) Now you've done it. You broke my tennis racket.

JENNIFER. And Mommy's new Mr. Coffee.

ALL. Oooh.

DANNY. (*off*) Now you're going to get it. Now you're really going to get it.

(*JENNIFER runs back onstage, followed by PAUL, then KATHY, then DANNY. PAUL wears a broken tennis racket around his neck, DANNY carries a broken handle. THEY each leap over the couch and*)

*run around the coffee table. As DANNY finally ap-
proaches them, KATHY restrains him again.)*

DANNY. How long have you two been fooling around?
JENNIFER. One week. That's all.
PAUL. One night. That's all.
JENNIFER. Ten minutes.
DANNY. That's all?
PAUL. *(correcting her)* One night!
KATHY. Ten minutes? You must have caught him on a
good night.
PAUL. Shut up Poot. Poot.
KATHY. Kill him, Danny.

*(DANNY advances, waving his broken handle like a
    sword. JENNIFER and PAUL run the opposite
    way, pushing KATHY down on the couch.)*

JENNIFER. I guess this isn't the best time to tell you,
Danny, but I want a divorce.
DANNY. That's why I'm killing you, Jennifer.
PAUL. It's all right, Jennifer. We'll die together.
JENNIFER. You're so brave.
PAUL. No, my legs are giving out.

*(PAUL holds up JENNIFER as a shield. KATHY
    restrains DANNY.)*

JENNIFER. Defend me, Paul.
DANNY. Stand still and fight like a man.
PAUL. Is that any way to talk to your wife?
DANNY. I'm talking to you. When I said "borrow

whatever you want for the weekend", I never thought you'd choose my wife.

PAUL. (*holding up chair lion-tamer style*) Sure, now you tell me.

DANNY. I don't want to kill you, Paul. But it's a matter of principle. I have to. It's nothing personal or anything.

PAUL. (*nobly setting chair down*) It's all right. I understand.

JENNIFER. I'm not a sex machine, Danny. You wanted a sex machine.

KATHY. What can I say? He finally got his wish.

JENNIFER. Paul isn't interested in sex.

(*PAUL does a take as KATHY laughs at him.*)

JENNIFER. Paul loves me for the person that I am.

DANNY. What's that? What is that? He loves you because you're a lying, cheating adulteress?

(*PAUL nods.*)

DANNY. You chippy.

PAUL. That does it. Nobody calls my woman a chippy.

DANNY. "Your woman?" "Your woman?" That woman is legally *my* woman.

JENNIFER. I'm not a piece of property, Danny.

DANNY. If you are, it's community property.

PAUL. She's not an item up for sale.

DANNY. That's 'cause she'd be in the used furniture department. Step outside, Chippy-Stealer!

(*DANNY points out the door and taps his feet. PAUL, defending JENNIFER's honor, heads for the door*)

*in an exaggerated macho walk. As HE approaches
the door, HE backs up to his first position.*)

PAUL. (*scared*) There's a bear outside!

DANNY. Oh, chicken, huh? I say we step outside and
settle this like two mature rational adults. To the death.
What do you say, "Ten Minute Man."

PAUL. (*his manhood assaulted*) Okay. For you, Jennifer.
And for my honor (*pushing the broken stem of the racket
over his shoulder*) as a man.

(*KATHY laughs at him. HE shoots her a look, then
proceeds to walk a "manly" walk towards the front
door.*)

DANNY. This should take about ten minutes. Kathy.

(*PAUL stops in his tracks. HE proceeds again towards
the door.*)

DANNY. After you, Wife-Coveter! What are you waiting
for?

(*PAUL turns and "manly" walks up to DANNY.*)

PAUL. (*scared*) I don't trust you. You're going to lock
me outside with the bear!

DANNY. We have been best friends for fifteen years.
When I say I'm stepping outside . . . I'm stepping outside!

(*PAUL and DANNY roll up their sleeves, hitch up their
pajamas and robe belts, turn and walk "manly"
walks out the front door. DANNY, however, steps
back in and locks the door behind PAUL.*)

JENNIFER. Danny!
PAUL. (*off*) YOU SON OF A BITCH!
DANNY. Sucker!
PAUL. Let me in!
JENNIFER. Let him in.
DANNY. Let the bear eat him.
KATHY. Eat him, bear!

(*PAUL screams for them to let him in, in front of the window. HE turns and sees something horrible. HE points off and runs the opposite direction. DANNY ignores this and advances on JENNIFER.*)

DANNY. And now for you, Miss Behind-My-Back.
JENNIFER. (*standing her ground*)Danny, I want a divorce.
KATHY. I think you're a little late, Jen.

(*KATHY & JENNIFER gasp. For, at the window we see BILL – naked, with the exception of bushes HE has fastened around himself like a thick grass skirt. His Marine hat is twisted on his head and sprigs of greens are in his hair. HE points off and screams for them to let him in.*)

BILL. Help! Let me in! Help!

(*KATHY opens the door and BILL flies in, out of breath, eyes wide with fear.*)

BILL. There's a bear out there! It's the meanest looking thing I ever saw!
DANNY. Where are your clothes?

BILL. He ate them. The bear ate my clothes.

DANNY. Right off your body?

KATHY. Where's Mommy?

BILL. She's chasing him around the yard with a rake. Stay where you are. I'll handle this. (*BILL dashes off into the bedrooms.*)

JENNIFER. We should do something.

DANNY. You're not going anywhere.

JENNIFER. Don't you hurt me.

DANNY. I'm not going to hurt you.

KATHY. Oh go ahead and hurt her.

JENNIFER. You shut up! You want him? You can have him. But I don't think you can take it. Here he is. Lock, Stock, and Ethel Merman Records.

DANNY. You make me sound like a monster. I have some good qualities, you know.

JENNIFER. You do? Like what?

DANNY. Well . . . I've never left the seat up!

KATHY. Wait a minute. Let me tell you something about your husband, little sister. You never realized how lucky you were.

DANNY. Yeah.

KATHY. He is the most compassionate, loving, giving, sexy, romantic man I've ever known.

DANNY. Yeah.

KATHY. And I've known a few.

DANNY. Yeah?

KATHY. However, if you ever start to treat me like Jennifer, you're a dead man.

DANNY. I never meant to hurt you, Jennifer.

JENNIFER. I think I meant to hurt you. But along the way, I found a man I really love. And I know he loves me.

DANNY. Paul?

JENNIFER. He'll make me happy.

DANNY. Yeah, but . . .

KATHY. He's a nice guy, Danny. He'll make her happy.

DANNY. Yeah, but . . .

KATHY. Congratulations, Jenny. I want to wish you the best of luck.

JENNIFER. Who's going to tell Daddy?

KATHY & JENNIFER. (*pointing to each other*) You.

DANNY. What does this do to the family album?

(*PAUL staggers in, in shock. Sprigs of greens stick out of his hair and pockets. His pajamas are disheveled and his sock hangs off.*)

JENNIFER. Paul! I almost forgot! Thank God.

KATHY. What's the matter with him?

DANNY. What's the matter with you, Paul?

JENNIFER. Are you all right?

PAUL. I'm going to be sick.

JENNIFER. Did you see the bear?

PAUL. I saw the bear.

JENNIFER. Did you see my mother?

PAUL. I'm going to be sick.

JENNIFER. Where's my mother?

PAUL. Running around the yard with a rake singing "Shine On Harvest Moon."

KATHY. What happened out there? Where's my mother?

PAUL. When you threw me outside, I saw this big hairy thing ripping clothes to shreds over by the sycamore tree. So I started to run for my car. Then I remembered your mother was over there. Mrs. Hogan was over there and I didn't want anything to happen to her. So I ran over to help her. But just as I approached the sycamore tree,

I realized there was nothing left. Just a pile of shredded clothes.

JENNIFER. Oh no.

DANNY. And what happened?

PAUL. Suddenly, out of the sky, came . . . your mother. Swinging on a rope. Brandishing a garden rake. Stark naked. That bear took off like a shot.

KATHY. Is Mommy all right?

PAUL. I don't know. I outran that bear halfway down the drive way.

(MARY enters, naked underneath her bush-dress. SHE carries a garden rake and is absolutely exuberant.)

KATHY. Mother!

MARY. Not bad for an old lady, huh, Paul?

PAUL. I didn't touch her.

KATHY. What are you wearing?

DANNY. Nice bush, you have there.

(BILL enters from the bedrooms, still in bush, Marine hat now replaced by a helmet. HE carries a gun.)

BILL. Stand back. I'll handle this.

PAUL. I didn't touch her!

DANNY. Look, His-n-Hers Hedges.

MARY. The bear is gone, Bill. I scared him away!

BILL. What did you do, make a pass at him, Mary?

DANNY. Are you all right?

PAUL. What happened out there?

MARY. Well . . .

BILL. Mary.

MARY. Now, Bill, these kids are adults. They can

handle it. Your father and I were out in the moonlight, doing what we love to do most.

(*The "kids" look at each other confused.*)

DANNY. Watching TV?

BILL. No.

MARY. We were pitching woo.

DANNY. Woo??

BILL. Shut up, you.

MARY. As I lay back on that grassy knoll behind the sycamore tree, your father began to lick my ear. Then I realized Bill was waving to me from across the yard. The next thing I knew, I was face to face with the foulest smelling breath I've ever encountered. It was like Uncle Kenny when he eats pastrami.

JENNIFER. Thank God you're all right.

BILL. Sure. Now that we have this. (*BILL pats his trusty rifle.*)

MARY. What an exciting anniversary. It'll be hard to top this next year.

KATHY. That's for sure.

MARY. I don't feel routine tonight, Bill.

BILL. Margaret never even made Jack go through a night like this.

MARY. What's everybody doing up?

DANNY. You wouldn't believe us if we told you.

BILL. A bear just ate my clothes. I'll believe anything.

KATHY. Well, we've got some good news and some bad news.

PAUL. If you'll excuse me, I have to go to the bathroom.

BILL. Again?

JENNIFER. You're not going anywhere.

BILL. What's the bad news?

JENNIFER. Danny and I are getting a divorce.

(DANNY hides behind KATHY. JENNIFER hides behind PAUL.)

BILL. What's the bad news?

MARY. Oh, you're not. Oh, why? Oh, why? First Margaret and Jack and now this. Oh. You can't divorce Jennifer, Danny. You're part of the family. You're family.

BILL. Mary, mind your own business.

KATHY. Don't worry, Mom. Danny will still be part of the family.

MARY. That's impossible. If Jennifer and Danny get a divorce, how can he be part of the family unless . . . .

(MARY & BILL look to their right and see JENNIFER & PAUL as a couple. THEY look to their left and see DANNY & KATHY as a couple. THEY look to each other and then out front.)

MARY. Oh no. Oh no!

BILL. You mean you and he and you and him have been . . . and you're going to . . . but first you want to . . . and then you're still going to . . .

DANNY. Something like that.

BILL. And you're still my son-in-law? Give me the gun, Mary!

MARY. Bill.

KATHY. Daddy!

MARY. Bill. Calm down. Don't hurt the children.

BILL. It's not for them, Mary. It's for you. You raised them, didn't you?

JENNIFER. We just want to be happy.

BILL. Happy? You don't know what "happy" is.

MARY. I do.

BILL. So do I.

MARY. Margaret and Jack did.

PAUL. Who are Margaret and Jack?

KATHY. What happened to them?

MARY. Well . . .

BILL. Nevermind. Mary, go put your robe on. Your leaves are shedding.

JENNIFER. Don't you want me to be happy, Daddy?

BILL. I let you marry him, didn't I? What do you think? Marriage is a joke? A couple of years go by, you have a few problems and you move on? (*BILL begins addressing the troops.*) Marriage is work. Work, Paul. One's job or occupation. That which is produced by thought and effort. You got that?

PAUL. Yessir.

BILL. I can't hear you.

PAUL. YESSIR.

BILL. Hard work. And you're all going to work at it. You got that?

ALL. Yessir.

BILL. I can't hear you.

ALL. YESSIR.

BILL. Marriage is no picnic. Marriage is no party. Marriage is not pretty. It's work. Hard work. Some years are great . . . Some years are terrible . . .

(*MARY nods.*)

BILL. And some years are stuck in the middle somewhere.

MARY. We've been in the middle seven years now.

BILL. Enjoy it while it lasts, Mary. You kids don't know what "happy' is. But your mother and I do. And do you know why? Because we lasted. Thirty years . . .

ALL. Twenty-nine years.

BILL. Same thing. Twenty-nine of the best years a man could ask for. And do you know why? Because we spent them together.

MARY. Oh, Bill . . . it's nice to be a novelty.

CURTAIN

PROPERTY LIST

ACT ONE

PRE-SET:
  AT BED
    Five bedspreads made up over one another, to be peeled off after each scene.
  NIGHT TABLE
    Telephone
  DOOR KNOB
    "Do Not Disturb" sign
  DRESSER
    Charlie perfume
  OFF R (CLOSET in SCENE FOUR)
    Tennis racket
  SOUND
    "Back to Bataan" tape rewound and cued, TV screen blue light

PERSONAL PROPS

DANNY – Watch, scrap of paper in jacket pocket, corset in gift box, bowling ball, suitcase with clothing to pack.

KATHY – Shoulder bag, scarf, red wig, suitcase with clothing to pack, corset in gift box.

JENNIFER – Sunglasses, hat, watch, pocketbook.

PAUL – Sunglasses, clip-on mustache, hat, watch.

BILL – Marine hat.

MARY – Laundry basket with blue and brown socks, suitcase filled with clothes.

INTERMISSION

Replace bed with couch and coffee table, remove Act One curtains to reveal Act Two drapes and picture window, set wall hangings and throw pillows.

ACT TWO

PRE-SET:
  COFFEE TABLE
    Greeting card with photograph on front, floral arrangement.
  BAR
    Filled bottles of white wine, club soda, ginger ale, scotch and vodka, filled ice bucket with lid, four wine glasses.
  OFF R
    Bill's tie, battle helmet, rifle, lipstick.

OFF L
  Sandwich, crash-box, broken tennis racket frame,
  broken tennis racket handle.
OFF U.S.R.
  Bill's bush costume, Mary's bush costume, rake, extra
    sprigs of greens.

PERSONAL PROPS

BILL — Marine hat

JENNIFER — Wrapped Mr. Coffee box.

DANNY — Suitcase (from 1-4), watch, corsage box —
  smashed on one side, containing smashed corsage.

KATHY — Wrapped corset box.

PAUL — Blindfold, Kathy's suitcase (1-5), tennis racket.

SCENE CHANGE BETWEEN 2-1 AND 2-2

Strike all presents and suitcases, set tennis racket by bar.

COSTUME PLOT

KATHY

SCENE ONE: Hot pink blouse, black slit skirt, black heels, print scarf around neck, corset and black stockings underneath.

SCENE FIVE: Violet dress, heels.

ACT TWO – SCENE ONE: Blue skirt, blue blouse, heels.

SCENE TWO: Corset and black stockings under green wrap-around robe, black heels.

DANNY

SCENE ONE: Three-piece suit, pink shirt, tie, black shoes, black socks, red and white striped boxer shorts.

SCENE FOUR: Work shirt, blue cords, yellow cardigan sweater, Hush Puppies.

ACT TWO – SCENE ONE: Beige dress pants, white shirt, black V-neck sweater, beige shoes.

SCENE TWO: Red bathrobe, blue print boxers, T-shirt, black socks.

JENNIFER

SCENE TWO: Blue print blouse, blue slit skirt, trenchcoat, wide-brim hat, sunglasses, heels, camisole underneath.

SCENE FIVE: Green dress, heels.

ACT TWO – SCENE ONE: Red sleeve-less dress, heels.

SCENE TWO: Flannel nightgown, robe, slippers.

PAUL

SCENE TWO: Grey pants, blue print shirt, Blue V-neck sweater, trenchcoat, black slip-on shoes, sunglasses, wide-brim hat, clip-on mustache.

SCENE FOUR: Jeans, grey shirt, red windbreaker, Topsiders.

ACT TWO – SCENE ONE: Pink shirt, tie, grey pants, sports jacket, dress shoes.

SCENE TWO: Plaid pajamas (three sizes too small – or too big depending on the size of the actors playing PAUL & BILL), black socks.

MARY

SCENE THREE: Orange flannel bathrobe, slippers, orange scarf tied in hair.

ACT TWO – SCENE ONE: Mint-green pant suit, jewelry.

SCENE TWO: Leopard bathrobe, neutral Danskin underneath.

into:
    Bush costume.

BILL

SCENE THREE: Plaid bathrobe, Marine Flight Hat (beige), white socks.

ACT TWO – SCENE ONE: T-shirt, work pants, brown shoes, white socks, Marine hat.
    into:
        Loud yellow and blue striped tie.

SCENE TWO: Plaid bathrobe, neutral Danskin underneath, Marine hat.
    into:
        Bush costume, Marine hat – worn sideways with sprigs of green sticking out of it,
    add:
        Battle helmet in place of Marine hat.

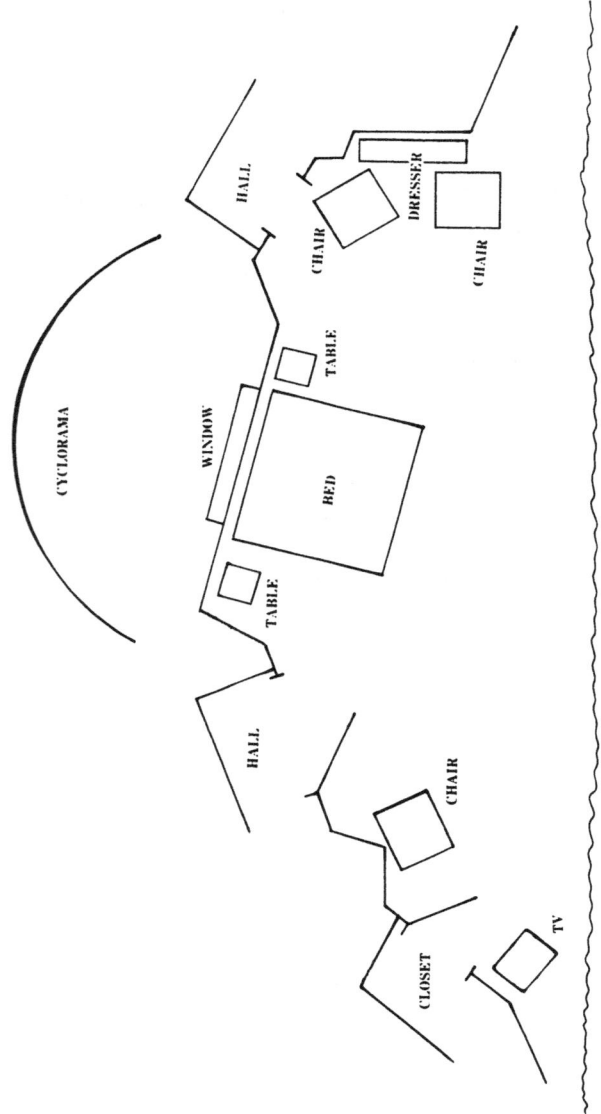

—Set Design—
Having A Wonderful Time. Wish You Were Her
Act 1

106

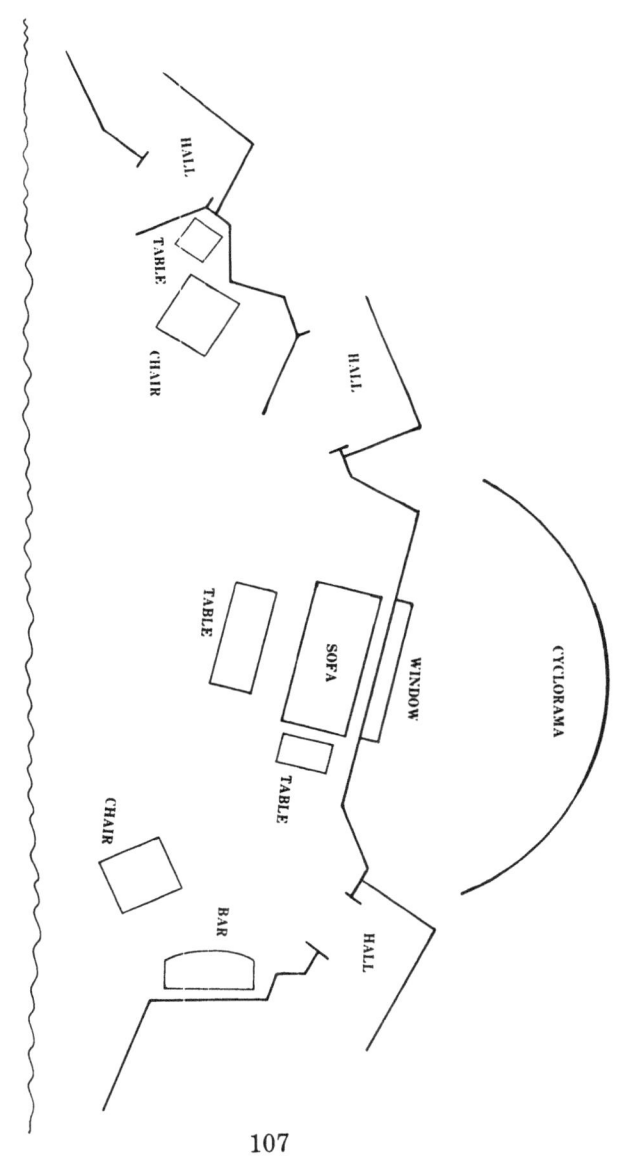

—Set Design—
Having A Wonderful Time, Wish You Were Here
Act II

Also By

Billy Van Zandt
and
Jane Milmore

BATHROOM HUMOR

DROP DEAD!

INFIDELITIES

A LITTLE QUICKIE

LOVE, SEX, AND THE IRS

PLAYING DOCTOR

THE SENATOR WORE PANTYHOSE

SUITEHEARTS

WHAT THE BELLHOP SAW

YOU'VE GOT HATE MAIL

OTHER TITLES AVAILABLE FROM SAMUEL FRENCH

THE DECORATOR
Donald Churchill

Comedy / 1m, 2f / Interior
Marcia returns to her flat to find it has not been painted as she
arranged. A part time painter who is filling in for an ill colleague
is just beginning the work when the wife of the man with whom
Marcia is having an affair arrives to tell all to Marcia's husband.
Marcia hires the painter a part time actor to impersonate her
husband at the confrontation. Hilarity is piled upon hilarity
as the painter, who takes his acting very seriously, portrays the
absent husband. The wronged wife decides that the best revenge
is to sleep with Marcia's husband, an ecstatic experience for
them both. When Marcia learns that the painter/actor has slept
with her rival, she demands the opportunity to show him what
really good sex is.

"Irresistible."
– London Daily Telegraph

"This play will leave you rolling in the aisles....
I all but fell from my seat laughing."
– London Star

OTHER TITLES AVAILABLE FROM SAMUEL FRENCH

CAPTIVE
Jan Buttram

Comedy / 2m, 1f / Interior

A hilarious take on a father/daughter relationship, this off beat comedy combines foreign intrigue with down home philosophy. Sally Pound flees a bad marriage in New York and arrives at her parent's home in Texas hoping to borrow money from her brother to pay a debt to gangsters incurred by her husband. Her elderly parents are supposed to be vacationing in Israel, but she is greeted with a shotgun aimed by her irascible father who has been left home because of a minor car accident and is not at all happy to see her. When a news report indicates that Sally's mother may have been taken captive in the Middle East, Sally's hard-nosed brother insists that she keep father home until they receive definite word, and only then will he loan Sally the money. Sally fails to keep father in the dark, and he plans a rescue while she finds she is increasingly unable to skirt the painful truths of her life. The ornery father and his loveable but slightly-dysfunctional daughter come to a meeting of hearts and minds and solve both their problems.

OTHER TITLES AVAILABLE FROM SAMUEL FRENCH

TAKE HER, SHE'S MINE
Phoebe and Henry Ephron

Comedy / 11m, 6f / Various Sets
Art Carney and Phyllis Thaxter played the Broadway roles of parents of two typical American girls enroute to college. The story is based on the wild and wooly experiences the authors had with their daughters, Nora Ephron and Delia Ephron, themselves now well known writers. The phases of a girl's life are cause for enjoyment except to fearful fathers. Through the first two years, the authors tell us, college girls are frightfully sophisticated about all departments of human life. Then they pass into the "liberal" period of causes and humanitarianism, and some into the intellectual lethargy of beatniksville. Finally, they start to think seriously of their lives as grown ups. It's an experience in growing up, as much for the parents as for the girls.

"A warming comedy. A delightful play about parents vs kids. It's loaded with laughs. It's going to be a smash hit."
– *New York Mirror*